TOTAL IMMERSION
An Academic Thriller
Sid Stark
Helia Press

I0544182

Want to keep in touch and hear about news and special offers first? Sign up for my mailing list and get your FREE novella by scanning the QR code below:

1

IT WASN'T THE BROKEN plate that smashed everything.

No, those fault lines had been running through us and between us from the very beginning. Tearing us apart, even when it felt like they were pulling us together. Their tremors had been with us from the start, threatening our foundations. The signs had been plain to see, if we had cared to look. But we had been willfully blind to the signals, taking the seismic foreshocks as evidence of rising passion, not an oncoming tidal wave.

"Erin's missing," Alex said.

He was frowning as he said it, a sharp crease between his eyebrows. Normally Alex Miller, my almost-fiancé, looked a good ten years younger than his actual age of thirty-nine. His face was thin and, when he was happy, boyishly expressive, with hazel eyes full of that light of intelligence that's more attractive than mere good looks.

But right now worry was adding lines to his face, and that light of intelligence was turned away from me, along with his eyes. Not because he was afraid of how I might react to yet another conversation about his ex-girlfriend who was back in his life in a bigger and bigger way. Because he was much more concerned about Erin than he was about me. At least, that's how it felt.

"How long's she been gone?" I asked.

I was proud of how calm my voice was. I thought I sounded sympathetic and supportive, not at all like a woman on the verge of screaming and throwing crockery at the person I had convinced myself I wanted to spend the rest of my life with.

"She didn't show up at work this morning," Alex said. "And she hasn't answered her phone all day."

"Doesn't she go AWOL pretty regularly?" I was pretty sure I managed to keep my voice warm, sympathetic, and non-judgmental. But it was hard.

Alex had started a hot and very heavy affair with Erin Carver when they had been serving together in the Navy. It had been, I had gathered, one of those lightning-strike, once-in-a-lifetime loves. Or it least it had been for him. I had originally thought it had been for her, too. But the more I watched her, the less I thought she had ever actually loved him. After spending a summer seeing her interact with him on a regular basis, I was starting to suspect that she had always just been using him as a shield to hide from her own problems.

My suspicions were strengthened by the fact that their great love had collapsed under the weight of Erin's extreme, deep-seated fucked-upness. This had caused her to drink, sleep around, and disappear for weeks at a time. During my more judgmental moods, I thought that this was not how you treated someone you really loved. They shouldn't be just another drug that you used to dull the pain. Or perhaps for someone like Erin, the drugs you used to dull the pain were what you loved most in life. You still used them, though, and then threw them away when you were done with them.

Erin wasn't quite ready to throw Alex away yet, though. Or maybe there was still some tie between them they couldn't break, possibly a karmic one. After cutting off all contact with each other for years, they had both ended up at the DLI, the Defense Language Institute in Monterey, California, and were now working together closely. I liked to tell myself it didn't bother me. More and more, I was realizing I was lying.

Under other circumstances it could have been okay. Alex and Erin had broken up a long time before he and I had gotten together, while we had both been adjuncting in New Jersey. Our relationship had continued when I'd moved first to North Carolina, then back to my alma mater Indiana University, and then to Georgia, in pursuit of contingent faculty jobs, and he'd taken a job teaching Arabic at the DLI. Now I was spending the summer with him in Monterey teaching an intensive Russian course at the nearby civilian institute. Everything should have been hunky-dory.

Or so I was trying to tell myself. Alex was very demonstrably with me now, and Erin was with someone else too, another ex-servicemember named Frank McAvoy who'd taken a shine to her when all three of them had been in Iraq, and had taken his chance when they'd both ended up in Northern California.

We'd all tried to act like two normal couples who had a lot in common and enjoyed spending time together. Frank was now with the FBI and had offered to try and help me get a job there myself. Then I could leave my precarious job in Georgia, maybe move out to Northern California with Alex, and all four of us could live in peace and harmony and happily ever after.

The problem was, Alex and I both disliked Frank. I kind of suspected Erin did too, she was just even better at lying to herself than I was. Or maybe she just didn't know how to be with someone she really loved. Maybe she'd never really loved someone at all. Maybe she wasn't capable of it. Or maybe she had an even more tragic backstory than I knew. To my critical eyes, that didn't make her any less of a user.

In any case, Alex and Erin's hot and heavy affair was still casting long shadows over both of them. And then, this past May, Frank had shot Erin.

The story was that it was a stupid accident. They'd been doing some target practice together. Somehow, he'd accidentally fired a loaded handgun into her left side at point-blank range.

Fortunately, it had missed everything vital. Her heart and lungs were fine. So, she'd told me in one of the weirdly intimate conversations we'd been having recently, was her left breast. There had been some concern there would be permanent scarring and distortion. But everything was healing up nicely. She'd lifted up her shirt and shown me before I could stop her.

"This is different," Alex said, interrupting unwelcome memories of the pink healing scar on the smooth pale skin covering Erin's left breast. I didn't particularly care to look at other women's breasts. I especially didn't care to look at Erin's, since she and I were disturbingly alike. Clearly Alex had a type, because we were both slender and athletic, with the dark hair, blue eyes, and pale skin of a Celtic maiden in a BBC drama. Alex, it had to be said, was not alone in having that type, because we both got plenty of attention from most men and some women. I was six inches taller than Erin's 5'4", able to look Alex and most other men in the eye, but other than that, we could have been sisters.

So all in all, I had not been pleased when Erin had shown me her breasts. I would have said that was from my jealousy and my deeply rooted heterosexuality. I had a suspicion some of my friends would tell me it was from deeply repressed lesbian tendencies. I was 99% sure that was the kind of liberal academic bullshit that won us so few friends and allies out in the "real world." 1% of me thought it might be true. Realistically, I was probably a 1, maybe a 2, on the Kinsey Scale. But that was normal, right? And it didn't matter anyway because I had Alex. I would never have to dive into the anguish and heartbreak that was same-sex dating. If things worked out the way I hoped they would, I would never have to dive into the anguish and heartbreak that was any kind of dating ever again. Right? *RIGHT?*

"How is it different?" I asked. From Alex's sudden look my way, I guessed that my voice had lost a lot of its former warmth and sympathy, and the underlying fear and anger was starting to show through.

"Erin wouldn't miss work," Alex said. "She'd cheat on me and leave me hanging, but she wouldn't fuck around where work was concerned. That was the only thing she could ever be counted on to show up for."

"Uh-huh," I said. I resisted the temptation to point out that Erin couldn't cheat on Alex now, since they weren't together. I knew what he was trying to say. And I also knew that in his mind, maybe they always would be a little bit together. I told myself that was okay. After all, I had someone I'd always be a little bit together with too. I should be more understanding.

"Should we drive up to Salinas and check on her?" I asked.

Alex's face relaxed into a relieved smile. "Yeah," he said. "That's a great idea." He looked at his phone, checking the time and probably for any text notifications. "Maybe we should go ahead and go," he said. "If you don't mind. We can grab something on the way if you're hungry."

I was starving. I was also trying to put myself on a diet. "That's okay," I said. "Let's check on Erin first, and then figure out what we want to do. Maybe she just has the flu and her phone died, or something. We can bring her some soup and hit up a restaurant in Salinas before heading back."

"Great idea. And Rowena?" An expression that was equal parts grateful appreciation and shameful guilt crossed Alex's face. "Thanks. I know this isn't how you wanted to spend your summer, and especially not your last weekend here in California."

"No problem," I said. "Let's get going."

2

ALEX WAS PAYING $1,500 a month for a crappy one-bedroom apartment amongst the strip malls, dollar stores, and fast-food joints on Casanova Avenue in Monterey. The only redeeming feature about it was that he had a ten-minute drive to work. Erin had inherited a detached house in Salinas, half an hour away. To my eyes, it was also a fairly crappy house, although admittedly nicer than anywhere I had ever lived. But property values on the California coast were so ridiculously high that even a two-bedroom, one-bathroom ranch-style house that looked like it could be blown away in a stiff breeze was worth a cool half million. It was one of the many strokes of good fortune Erin appeared to have gotten in her life. Too bad none of that stopped her from being a fucked-up mess. I guess money really can't buy you love. Of course, my own experience was that virtuous poverty was no guarantee, either.

"I'm really fucking sorry," Alex said for the third time as we drove north up Route 1, the highway that ran up most of California's scenic but dangerous coast, in his piece-of-shit—his words—Nissan Sentra.

I had offered to drive my own equally shitty Honda Civic, but Alex had said the hideous grinding noise that had emanated from the gear box the last time I had tried to shift into second in his presence had put him off it, and he wasn't going to get into it again until I had it worked on. Then we had argued for a while about the advisability of me setting off on a cross-country drive in it on Sunday. The argument had ended in a truce when we'd both realized that neither of us had the money to get it fixed. I was just going to pray as hard as I could to whatever kindly disposed supernatural powers happened to be looking my way that I made it back to Georgia.

"There's no need," I reassured him. Again. I was getting pretty tired of this reassurance shit. I was starting to be haunted by the suspicion that I was being forced to make him feel better about his guilt for doing wrong by me. And I was starting to resent that, and that was making *me* feel guilty. I had imbibed enough of the expectations of saintly womanhood while living in Russia to feel bad about not being able to comfort my man when he was being racked by pangs of conscience for mistreating me. I should be all-forgiving, right? Or at least, I shouldn't be so upset about this, right? All couples went through hard times, right? Getting through them and reaffirming your commitment to each other was part of what made you stronger. *RIGHT?*

I realized I had said *RIGHT* to myself at least six times in the past half-hour. I needed a distraction.

"Do you mind if I put on some music?" I asked.

"Go right ahead." Alex sounded relieved to have an excuse to be generous. "Whatever you like."

I brought out my phone and opened the music app. In a moment that even in my current funk I recognized as marvelously, gloriously ironic, Florence + the Machine's "You've Got the Love" came on.

"What do you think is going on with Erin?" I said. Loudly, in order to drown out the lyrics about transcendent love.

Alex shrugged, his eyes fixed on the road ahead. "She's been going through a rough patch right now."

"That's understandable," I said, although in my heart of hearts, I thought that after three months, it was high time for Erin to pull herself out of her rough patch.

"It's not just the...you know. Getting shot. It's...well...some stuff might be getting out. Bad stuff. About her. About what she did. About what *we* did. In Iraq."

"Uh-huh?" I said. I tried to think of a way to ask, delicately and sensitively, if this was about the torture program at the black site Erin, Alex, and Frank had all apparently been involved in. I didn't know the details. I didn't *want* to know the details. I'd spent a lot of time in my previous career in a human rights NGO working with torture victims. I could fill in the details pretty well myself. I would just substitute waterboarding, the US's current preferred method of torture, for electrocution, the method favored by Russian forces.

Alex had confessed his involvement with this particularly unsavory aspect of the current War on Terror to me last semester. He'd said that he'd mainly been responsible for processing the paperwork, which I believed. He said he was tormented by guilt about it, which I also believed. Only a guilty conscience could make someone act as badly as he had towards me. He was now trying to seek redemption. Unfortunately, his attempts at seeking redemption had thus far not made either of us any happier.

"It's..." He blew out a big breath. "It's just so fucked up, Rowena. As you know. And...I fucking hate how it's pulling me back into all that shit. I fucking *hate* that I'm spending your last weekend here in California chasing after Erin and dealing with our dirty past."

"It's okay," I said. "It needs to be done." In another moment of delicious irony, "I'm Not Calling You a Liar" came on. Jesus Christ. I was seriously starting to rethink my fondness for this album and for Florence + the Machine in general. But shutting it off now seemed too obvious. I would have to sit through it and hope that shuffle would choose something less apropos for the next song.

"Someone's been digging stuff up," Alex was saying. "Some fucking journalist. Why the fuck can't they let things lie? Why the fuck do they have to go poking their noses into absolutely fucking everything?"

"Well," I said. "You know. Accountability. Transparency. Freedom of speech. All that."

"Yeah. Sounds great until it's fucking aimed at *you*." Alex slouched down in his seat, not looking at me. I couldn't tell if he was in a general snit, or a specific snit aimed at me.

I had never been a journalist. But I had been engaged to one. Just like Alex had had a lightning-strike love with another person, so had I. Mine was with the Russian investigative journalist Dima Kuznetsov. Very good-looking. Very driven, especially when it came to exposing crime, corruption, and evil-doing. Maybe because there was a fair amount of crime, corruption, and evil-doing in his own backstory. So much, in fact, that he'd sent me away in order to keep me safe from all the darkness and danger that followed him around.

I had not been happy about that decision. But I hadn't been able to do anything about it. Not only was Dima very, very, *very* fucked up, he always, always, *always* got his own way. Maybe that was why Alex's problems had snuck under my radar at first. My dosimeter for troubled souls was set to such a high level that Alex had seemed normal and healthy. Sadly, that was turning out not to be true.

Anyway, I couldn't tell right now if Alex's anger at journalists was just because they were causing trouble for Erin, or from repressed jealousy of Dima. He'd told me several times that he didn't begrudge me my past or resent Dima for the part he'd played in it. The first time we'd had that conversation, it had probably been healthy and smart. The next time had maybe been a little less healthy and smart. The last time we'd had it, which had been just yesterday after Dima had texted me in the middle of dinner and I'd stopped talking to Alex to answer him, should perhaps have been a major red flag.

"So apparently this journalist is planning to write, like, a whole fucking book on the US program of, well..." Alex said.

"'Enhanced interrogation?'" I suggested, when he trailed off, unable to get the words out.

"Yeah. That shit. And somehow she found out about Erin, and now she's all hot to talk to her. To get a 'woman's perspective' on the issue, let her tell her side of the story. It *sounds* all fucking noble and great. But it'll tear Erin apart. The whole thing...the whole thing was so...it was so..."

He swallowed and scrubbed at his face, his hand rasping on the stubble that he hadn't bothered to shave for the past couple of days. The slanting light of the setting sun made his light brown hair turn golden. It also lit up the gray patch on his cheek that had driven him to start shaving again last year, after half a decade of flirting with civilian scruffiness. But these past few weeks he'd stopped caring about that kind of thing. Shaving had been spotty at best. Meals had gone forgotten unless I reminded him. Laundry had only happened because I'd done it.

That made me mad, but it also made me want to lay my hand on his cheek and let the comfort flow from my skin to his. He was suffering, and I hated to see him suffer. I wanted to ride in on a white horse, my armor shining in the sun, and sweep him off his feet and carry him off into the sunset, to where he'd live happily ever after and never hurt again.

I was aware that many people would tell me that was wrong. My involvement with fucked-up men had driven me to occasional dives into self-help literature, which had told me that wanting to save people when they were in pain was not altruism and nobility of soul, but a pathological sign of a troubled childhood. According to the gurus, instead of helping each other out, we're supposed to pay professionals $50 an hour to polish us up so we can present nothing but our perfect selves to the world.

Or in other words, we're supposed pay strangers to tell us true love is a pathology and we need to learn to be more selfish. To me, it sounded like part of the American ideal of boring, sanitized, micromanaged, meaningless lives. Plus, my own savior fantasies combined both masculine and feminine gender roles in a way that probably meant I was supposed to declare myself to be nonbinary, or something. Too bad I was unequivocally 100% female, if currently wondering exactly where I fell on the Kinsey Scale.

But it was also true that my intense need to help others had gotten me into fairly biggish trouble on more than one occasion. And right now it looked to be well on the way to breaking my heart. Again.

"Erin was just in such a shitty position," Alex said. "You know how it is. If a woman refuses to torture and kill, then she's a girly-girl wimp who can't be counted on. If she agrees to torture and kill, then she's a monster, a hundred times worse than a man who does the same thing. It's the old lose-lose.

"And it wasn't like the people she was questioning were such angels. You hear all these stories about how the prisoners in Abu Ghraib and GTMO and so on were mainly innocent, and that's true. And you hear all these stories about how they were decent, good-hearted people. And maybe they were—to other men. But to women they were monsters. Maybe they weren't all terrorists, but to women, they were just about as bad. The female MPs who were guarding them—they'd come off shift shaking with fear and rage from all the rape threats and shit they were getting, all day, every day. And then they'd have to hide it from the men in their units, because admitting it would make them look weak. The only person they could tell was Erin. So she had good reason to want to hurt those men we were holding. I'm not saying what happened there was good. But I can understand why she did what she did.

"But if it all came out, you know what would happen. The men who gave the orders, and the men who carried them out, will get forgiven, and Erin will get crucified because she was the only woman and so she'll have to shoulder all the moral burden and be the target for all the moral outrage, even though she was the most junior person involved. And she really wants to turn her life around, make up for what she's done, and she needs a friend to help her out while she tries to do that, someone who at least has an inkling of what she's going through. I *can't* walk away from her right now, Rowena. Surely you understand that."

"I understand that," I said. And I did. It just didn't stop me from being gnawed by jealousy.

My phone started playing "Kiss With a Fist." Oh God. I'd never cared for this song about dysfunctional, abusive relationships. Now it seemed liked the shuffle algorithm was just playing with me.

The *ping* of an incoming text provided a welcome interruption. I checked my notifications. It was a message. From Dima.

3

DARLING INNOCHKA, it said. *Are you busy right now?*

I glanced over at Alex. Then I wished I hadn't. I was certain that my look had been furtive and guilty. But Alex was staring at the road ahead, deliberately, it felt, not catching my eye.

Why? I asked.

No reason. Just wanted to chat))))

Are you back from the front? Dima had spent the past two and a half years reporting from the front lines of the war in the Donbass. His idea of proper war correspondence involved being actually under fire as much as possible. Last week he had reported from a series of firefights around the embattled city of Avdiivka (or Avdeyevka, as us Russian speakers would say). Then he had gone silent for several days.

I had told myself it wasn't because he'd been killed. I had also told myself it wasn't because he was with Polya, the girl—she was apparently at least ten years his junior—a friend had set him up with, and who he kept talking about marrying. I had also told myself that him getting married should make me happy. That had maybe been the biggest lie I'd told myself so far.

Sort of. In Donetsk now. Thinking about going home.

Home to Moscow? I asked.

Yes. Mama's not doing so good. They're talking about a transplant.

Already? Galina Ivanovna, Dima's mother and my almost-mother-in-law, had been suffering from increasingly severe kidney disease the past few years. Most of the doctors she'd seen said there was little that could be done. A doctor herself, she had resigned herself to the situation a while ago. Dima was less resigned. Dima, I gathered from reading between the lines, was in a state of furious, burning despair. Especially since he thought that one of the reasons treatment options were so limited was because of him. The mother of Dima Kuznetsov, the oppositionist who occupied a special position at or near the top of the Kremlin's list of Journalists We'd Like to Kill, was getting turned away by every clinic in Moscow.

A colleague she trusted had told her that her only hope was either a transplant or enrollment in a clinical trial for some of the experimental treatments being developed. Transplants were hard to get and came with a lot of risks and problems. Clinical trials weren't risk-free either, and all the ones she'd identified as being useful were in the West. So she'd been waiting and hoping for a stroke of luck. Unfortunately, it seemed her time was running out.

Yes. Already. Inna, I need your help.

Of course. I wrote the reply so fast it felt like I'd sent it through telepathy, not typing.

There's a clinical trial. In Atlanta. Atlanta is in Georgia, right? Near you?

Yes. The northern California evening air coming in through the cracked-open car window should have been cool enough to make me shiver, but instead I was sweating.

I've been trying to read about this trial, but you know my English isn't so good.

Dima had been studying English on and off since before I'd known him. But even when we'd been engaged and I, at least, had been seriously planning for him to come live in America, his heart hadn't been in it. He spoke a smattering of phrases he'd picked up from English-speaking war correspondents, but his ability to decipher the language of a clinical trial website was limited.

Can you read the website for me? he wrote. *And tell me if you think it's a good fit for mama? And what she has to do to get into it?*

Of course, I wrote again. *I'll do it tomorrow.*

Thanks, Innochka! You're a real angel)))))

I wanted to point out that my angelic nature hadn't done me much good when he'd unilaterally decided to end our engagement and send me home, but I didn't. I wanted to ask if Polya was equally angelic. I didn't do that either.

Say hi to Galina Ivanovna for me, I wrote. *And start looking into getting visas for both of you.*

Both of us?

You're not going to send her to America by herself, are you?

I can't go to America.

Why not? I asked.

I've got stuff to do.

I thought about asking what stuff he had to do that could possibly be more important than his mother's life. I decided that wouldn't be very angelic, and more importantly, would make him angry and defensive. An angry and defensive Dima was a real pain in the ass and a major stumbling block towards anything other than confrontation and violence.

Okay, I wrote. *Send me the website and I'll take a look. And I'll also look into getting Galina Ivanovna a visa. Maybe they can expedite it for medical cases.* The wait time for Russian citizens to get a US visa—*if* they could—was a solid 6-8 months. Galina Ivanovna might not have that long. I had been suggesting to both of them that they get started on the process ever since the idea had first come up back in March. Now it was the first week of August and as far as I knew, they hadn't done anything to move things forward. I understood why they'd been dragging their feet. If I'd been in Galina Ivanovna's place, I couldn't say that I'd have done any different. But since I was in my place, it was a source of major frustration and stress for me.

Thank you, Innochka! And good night. Hugs.

4

"WHAT'S THE MATTER?"

I jumped. Alex was no longer staring straight ahead. We'd turned into the neighborhood where Erin lived, and he was looking at me out of the corner of his eye as we rolled slowly down the residential streets.

"Nothing." I shut off the music app, which had jumped to the next album and was now playing "Lover to Lover," and stuffed my phone back in my purse. That *hugs* was already burned into my retinas anyway. What, in God's good name, did Dima mean by that? Other than the obvious. And it was a common sign-off amongst Russians. All my female friends ended their emails and messages to me with it, and often threw in a few kisses as well. But Dima never had unless he'd really meant it.

"Is everything okay? Is it John?" Alex sounded genuinely concerned for me, in a way he hadn't for far too long.

"What? Oh, no, John's fine. As far as I know." John was my older brother. John was also a majorly fucked-up mess, as Alex had witnessed firsthand on more than one occasion. He could hold it together for work, but his personal life made Alex or Dima's seem tame and respectable by comparison. At least they weren't sleeping with a different married woman every weekend.

That I knew of. I hated that that thought had just floated through my head. But I couldn't stop it from happening. Any more than I could stop the thought that now *I* was edging ever closer to being the cheater.

No, no, no!

"It was Dima," I said, as casually as I could. "Asking for help for his mother. He wants to see if she can get into a clinical trial in Atlanta. But he doesn't want to have to come to the US with her."

"Oh." There was a line between Alex's brows again. I couldn't even begin to guess everything he was thinking and feeling right now, other than it looked to be a sick mixture of worry, jealousy, and relief.

"Yeah. Anyway. It doesn't look like anyone's at Erin's house."

We were pulling up to it. There were no lights on inside, and no sign of her car in the driveway. Alex parked at the curb and called her. Nothing.

"Let's go knock on the door," he said after a moment of indecision. "Just in case…"

"Yeah," I said, before he could finish that thought. "Good idea."

The motion-sensor lights Erin had gotten installed when she'd moved in—yet another thing I knew about her that I didn't want to, as we careened ever closer to some kind of unwanted intimacy and even friendship—came on when we stepped onto the cracked strip of concrete that served as her front walk. But that was the only sign of life in the place. Alex knocked at the front door, at first softly, then hard enough to make the whole flimsy structure shake. No response.

"Why don't you try calling her again, and I'll scout around the outside," I suggested. "Maybe we'll get lucky, or maybe I'll hear her phone."

Alex nodded tightly. We didn't have to say that me hearing her phone would be a sign of something very bad. But if she was lying passed out or worse on her bedroom floor, we didn't want to just leave her there.

I started around the house. Erin's aunt had gone for minimal landscaping. There were a couple of spindly bougainvilleas along the right side of the house, and a lawn of extremely patchy grass. Erin had hired someone to come out and mow and prune earlier this summer, and called it a day for outdoor maintenance. It magnified the air of cheap neglect her house radiated. It also made things easier for me.

I heard Alex dial as I started down the space between the bougainvillea and the house. I pressed my ear against the glass of the first window as the phone started to ring. No answering ring from within the house greeted me. I stood on my tiptoes and tried to peer inside. The blinds were firmly shut.

The rest of the house was the same. All the blinds were drawn, with no sounds, lights, or motion from beyond them to suggest occupancy. Alex tried calling twice more, but we caught no sound of an answering ring inside.

"Either her phone's switched off, or she's gone," I said, when I met him back at the front door. "Given that her car's not here, I'd guess the latter."

"Yeah." Alex made a face. "I guess that's good news. Do you"—he made another face—"think we should go door-to-door, ask her neighbors if they've seen her?"

I looked up and down the street. It was a series of houses a lot like Erin's, only better maintained. A lower-middle-class neighborhood, but one that required a six-figure salary to live in. No one was out walking their dog or working in their garden or playing with their kids. I tried to remember if I'd ever seen anyone do any of those things here. Surely there were normal, nice people around who would have taken in interest in Erin's comings and goings. This neighborhood was of approximately the same socioeconomic class as the one where my grandparents lived in Macon, Georgia, and that one was always teeming with life. But here people mostly seemed to be at work or shut up inside their uninspiring houses. Or maybe the problem wasn't them. Maybe it was Erin. And me. Either way, going door-to-door didn't seem likely to get good results.

"What about her family?" I suggested. "Maybe we should start with them. Have any of them heard from her?"

Alex made an even unhappier face. "Erin doesn't get along with her family. She used to be close with her uncle on the Carver side of the family—you know: the state senator I told you about, the one who wants to get into Congress—and his son, but...well, she cut off all contact with them after she got back from Iraq. There was some bad shit...actually, there was some bad shit starting long before that, but it got even worse in Iraq...anyway. The important thing is that they're not close now. Her mother's sister, the one who gave her this house, was the only person she could stand after she got back, or who could stand her. I don't know if she's even still speaking to her parents. And I don't know how to contact them, anyway. I only met them once, and they made it clear I wasn't good enough for them. My dad was only a dean at a biggish university. We weren't actually *rich*, like the San Diego Carvers, with their multi-million-dollar businesses and their political connections."

"Okay," I said. "What about Frank?"

I had very little desire to contact Frank. Frank, I'd already decided, was Bad News. Frank, I suspected, had been careless intentionally at the shooting range. I didn't have anything to support that suspicion other than my own dislike of him, but my dislike of him was strong enough that I felt like it had to have some kind of basis in reality. I was astonished that Erin was not only in contact with him, but was still in a relationship with him.

Well, no, I wasn't. Erin seemed to be drawn to Bad News like moth to a flame. I would judge her more harshly for it if I weren't beginning to worry that I was the same. But at least my Bad News tended to be less of a blowhard.

"Yeah, I guess you're right. Maybe she just decided to run off for a weekend of fun and good times with Frank. It wouldn't be the first time she's run off for something like that—although like I said, she doesn't normally blow off work. Everything else, yes, but not work. Sometimes I think she should have stayed in the service. At least that way she had a little discipline holding her together. As soon as she got out, she just completely fell apart."

"Yeah," I said. "Do you want to call Frank, or shall I?"

I was not pleased about the fact that I now had Frank's number in my phone. He'd insisted on giving it to me so we could talk about work, if the results of the interview and language testing I'd done two months ago for the FBI came back favorable. Then he'd called and texted me a couple of times about non-work things in a way that looked innocent on the surface, but didn't feel innocent to me. Frank was a player, and just because he'd hooked up with Erin, and I was very clearly with Alex, didn't mean he didn't want to keep his hand in the game. I was pretty sure I wasn't able to keep my aversion towards him from showing, and that it only added fuel to the fire of his pursuit of me.

"I can do it."

I wanted to wimp out and let Alex make the call. But he looked so miserable as he made the offer that I found myself saying, "Why don't I do it while you go ask the neighbors if they've seen anything."

"Thanks." Alex gave me a grateful smile. Somehow it seemed like all the smiles he'd been giving me lately had been grateful ones, as if I could only ever do him harm or favors, not make him happy just by being me. Then he turned away and set off—far too eagerly, I thought—towards the nearest house, while I steeled myself for a conversation with Frank.

5

FOR A MOMENT I WAS tempted to take the chicken way out and text Frank rather than calling him. But it was a lot easier to lie over text than over the phone. If Erin was there with him, or he knew where she was, I'd be much more likely to find out if I called.

I brought up Frank McAvoy on my Contacts list, and hit "Call." One ring...two...three...four...maybe he wasn't going to answer the phone...

"Rowena? What's up?"

I suppressed a pang of disappointment and dislike. "Hi, Frank. I've, uh..." *Oh jeez! Why was I blanking on what to say now!?! It's not complicated! Spit it out!* I didn't have a lot of amazing talents, but I was a good talker under pressure. I'd put that to the test on numerous occasions, and always been impressed with my own quick thinking and fluency. But now I was tongue-tied.

"Well, don't just stand there doing heavy breathing in my ear," said Frank. "Give it to me." He chuckled.

Irritation loosened whatever had blocked me before. "Have you seen Erin today?" I asked.

"No, why? You two plan a girls' night out?" He chuckled again. "Getting yourselves all pretty for the barbecue tomorrow?"

"No." Frank had invited us to some kind of barbecue thing with friends from work on Saturday. It sounded dreadful to me, so I had blocked it from my memory, despite knowing it was a chance to make a good impression on people who could potentially be my own future colleagues. I was ambitious and career-minded—or just desperate—enough to go to something like that. I was not enough of a career woman to actually enjoy it.

"I haven't seen her all day," I told Frank. "And she didn't come into work, and she's not at her place, and neither is her car, and she's not answering the phone. You don't have any idea where she might be?"

There was a pause at the other end of the line. When Frank spoke again, his voice had lost all of its forced jocularity and the sexual innuendo that always seemed just a little bit false to me. "Where are you, Rowena?"

"I'm standing in front of her front door. Alex and I drove up this evening when she didn't show up to work this morning and didn't answer her phone all day. Her car's not in the drive and she didn't answer the door. There aren't any lights on, and we can't hear anything inside the house, including when we call her phone. Alex is asking the neighbors if they've seen anything, and I thought I'd call you and see if you'd heard anything from her."

There was another pause at the other end of the line. "Alex tell you...never mind."

"He said Erin might be in a little trouble," I said. "About, um, stuff that happened earlier. That there's a journalist looking into, uh, some stuff that Erin did that might not, um, look so good."

"Fucking journalists," said Frank. "Why can't they keep their fucking noses out of other folks' business?" The words came out like he was thinking of something else, and was letting his mouth run to cover up his real thoughts.

"Yeah," I said. "So, uh, you don't have any idea where she might be?"

"Not with me." Frank's voice was all business now. "I haven't heard from her all day. I've got some places I can check, though. And you said Miller's there with you?"

"Uh-huh." Alex was walking back from the neighbor's house, the set of his shoulders showing it had been a fruitless expedition.

"Erin used to go fucking off on drinking and sex binges whenever things got too hard for her," said Frank. "She never pulled any of that shit with me, but I know she did it to Miller all the goddamn time, starting when they were in ROTC together. And to hear her tell it, he'd always go running after her on rescue missions, and he's still fucking doing it. So he probably has a good idea of where she might go. Tell him to make a list of all her favorite places and start going through them one by one. Let me know what you find."

"Okay," I said. I wasn't thrilled about being ordered around by Frank. But I had to admit his plan was the best one we had at the moment. "What about you?" I asked.

"I told you. I've got places I can look too. Let's check back in at, say, 21:00? Then we can go from there, decide whether we need to pull an all-nighter or not." He hung up before I could object.

6

"WAS THAT FRANK? DOES he know anything?"

"He says he doesn't. He suggested you might know of, um, some places that Erin might go if she's, uh, feeling bad, and that we should check them out. And he said he knew of some places to check too. We're supposed to call back at nine to see if we've made any progress."

Alex checked his phone. "It's already almost seven. I bet you're starving."

"Well...yes."

"Can you make it till we get back to Monterey? Frank's idea isn't half bad, much as I fucking hate to admit it. And we could pick up some food while we trawl through bars, kill two birds with one stone."

"Sounds great."

"I'll just..." Alex fished in his pockets and came up empty. "Do you have any paper? I want to leave her a note in case she comes back before we find her."

I dug around in my purse for a while before coming up with an old envelope I'd been using for making grocery lists. The back was completely covered with reminders to buy bagels and coffee. The front was as yet unused. I tore it off, ripped out a clean square of paper from under the return address, and handed it to Alex, along with the cheap ballpoint pen I carried with me. The cheap ballpoint pen that was in imminent need of replacement, apparently, because Alex had to shake it a bunch of times before it would release its ink and allow him to write

Erin, Give me a call when you see this, Alex on it. He stuck it in the door jamb, where it rested precariously on the lock. Then we got in his car and set off back for Monterey.

7

"WHAT DO YOU THINK?" Alex asked when we were back on the highway, heading south. "Is she really with Frank and he's lying?"

"If he is, he's doing a good job of it," I said. "What do you think? Is he that good of a liar?"

Alex did a one-shoulder shrug while navigating around a car creeping along at 35 miles per hour in the right lane, belching ominous dark smoke. "Frank's a complicated dude. I mean, you wouldn't think it to look at him. Most of the time he acts like a dumbass whose only goal is to sexually harass as many women as possible. And I have to fucking say, I think that impression is not wrong. But underneath it all there's something cunning working away beneath that graying buzz cut. He got ahead pretty damn well when he was in the military, and it sounds like he's getting ahead pretty damn well now in the FBI. I think he's a dick who enjoys shoving his dickishness in everyone's face, but there's something real there, too, you know what I mean? Like he's not just an ugly face."

"Yeah," I said. "That is my impression too."

"But I don't know if he's a good liar or not. I've never actually seen him lie that I know of. He's more the type to brazen his way through any situation by shouting the truth as loud as he could. He never hid what he was doing back, you know..."

"Yeah," I said again. "I get that sense from him as well. And I really don't think he was lying. I think he was worried about Erin. Or worried about something, at any rate."

"Well, maybe he's right and we'll find her drunk off her ass on Alvarado Street or in front of the Presidio," said Alex.

"Do you think she'd do that? Get drunk where colleagues and students could see her?"

Alex made another one-shoulder shrug. "I wouldn't think so. Like I said, work is the one thing that's always held her together, and she cares a lot about what subordinates—you know, like students—think of her. Since she's girl, and she's short, and she's cute, she's always had to fight to be taken seriously. She'd get shitfaced and bang anything with a dick when she was hurting—but she'd do it where the people she wanted to impress couldn't see her do it. But I don't have any better guesses, so we'll start there and see what we find."

"Maybe someone will know something," I said encouragingly. "Maybe she just needed some space to get her head on straight, and she'll come back tonight, see your note, and give you a call before we get home."

"Maybe," said Alex.

8

WE STARTED AT DUFFY'S Tavern, a family-style restaurant and bar just outside the entrance to the Presidio, the garrison that housed the DLI and various other military offices. Erin was a regular, and the four of us had had dinner there the previous Friday to celebrate the end of my program. Because she was well known and because it was so close to work, Alex thought it unlikely that we'd find Erin there tonight, but maybe the staff would know something. In any case, we could get food while we fished for information.

As expected, there was no sign of Erin when we stepped inside. It was transitioning from families out for supper to singles, couples, and groups out for a low-key Friday night of drinking and socializing. Many of them sported neat buzz cuts (the men) or neat above-the-collar hairstyles (the women) and the casual, jovial air of command I associated with American military officers. Alex ran into three people he knew from work. None of them had seen or heard from Erin all day.

Our server, a college-age girl with dark brown hair, square features that hinted at Puebloan heritage, and a nametag with "Tori" written on it in block capitals letters, hadn't seen her all day either, although she remembered her well.

"Yeah, of course," she said. "She came in with you two last Friday, and she came in again with someone else this week. I think it was Wednesday?"

"Was it the same man she was with on Friday?" Alex asked.

Tori shook her head. "It was a woman. I'd never seen her before."

"Do you remember what she looked like?" Alex asked.

Tori wrinkled up her forehead. "She was older," she said. "Not, like, *old* old, but older. Older than you two, or Erin. Kind of like my mom's age? Like maybe fifty? She had this awful haircut. Like a mullet or something, and it was all big and poofy, but not in a good way, and she obviously hadn't had it colored in a while, 'cause I could see gray streaks all the way through it. I remember 'cause Erin's hair is always so nice."

That was true. Erin might be a hot mess on the inside, but she wore her sleek almost-black hair in a neat collar-length bob that managed to look both feminine and professional, and also vaguely military even though she was a civilian now.

"Anyway, I thought this woman might be, like, an aunt or something, even though they didn't look much alike, but she had that look, you know what I mean? Like someone's aunt. But she wasn't very nice to Erin." Tori scrunched up her nose. "I couldn't hear what they were saying, but it must have been real mean, 'cause Erin kept shaking her head, like she was getting more and more upset, and then she told the woman to go away—I heard her even though I was two tables over, and everyone on this side of the room turned to look at her—and then the woman got up and gave her a business card or something, and then she left, and I thought Erin was, like, going to cry or something."

I thought Alex would ask a follow-up question, but he just sat there looking like all the weight of the world was on his shoulders. I tried to think of some smart questions I could ask myself. "What did she do afterwards?" was what I came up with.

Tori frowned. "Erin, or the other woman?"

"Both," I said.

She shrugged. "The other woman went over to the bar and said she wanted to settle the bill. I had to go over and help with that. When I went back to the table, Erin was gone."

I glanced over at Alex. He was still sitting there like all the weight of the world was on his shoulders. "Do you remember anything more about the other woman?" I asked. "Did you, uh, I don't know, happen to see her credit card or anything?"

Tori giggled nervously. "Wouldn't that be, like, a violation of privacy or something?"

"I think you're okay as long as you don't give us her actual card number," I said. "The thing is"—I looked around and then leaned in towards Tori conspiratorially— "we're looking for Erin. We're worried about her. So anything you can tell us that might help us find her would be really useful."

Tori's eyes, lined with copious eyeliner and framed with heavily mascara-ed lashes, got big. "You think she's *kidnapped* or something?"

"No," I said, although now that she'd put the idea in my head I was starting to worry. "We think she might be...unhappy. We just want to check on her and make sure she's okay."

Tori's eyes widened even more. "You think she might, like, *hurt* herself or something?"

"No," I said soothingly, although now that thought was going to haunt me too. "We just want to, you know, check on her and make sure she's okay. Like, um, maybe this woman on Wednesday was giving her a hard time, and now she needs a friend to help her out. And we'd like to know who this woman is, too, in case..."

I trailed off, running out of ideas. But Tori was off and running anyway.

"Maybe she's, like, extorting money from her or something!" she said enthusiastically.

"Ummmm..." I said.

"I'll go get Zeke," she said.

Zeke turned out to be the bartender, who also handled the register. He had a full reddish-brown beard that balanced out his balding head, a build that suggested "bouncer" more than "bartender," and a shy smile whenever he had to interact with women.

"Sure, I remember Erin coming in on Wednesday," he said, not quite looking at me. "And yeah, it's like Tori said. She was with this woman we'd never seen in here before, and they had words, and the woman got up and paid at the bar and left, and Erin slipped out then too."

"Do you remember the woman's name?" I asked.

He crinkled up his forehead in an I'm-thinking-hard expression. "I think it started with an H?" He shrugged. "I can't remember anything more than that, I'm afraid."

"Could you, um...look at the credit card receipts?" I asked.

He shook his head. "That'd be, like, a major violation of privacy. And the manager'd have my head if he found out. Wish I could help out more."

"Oh," I said. "Well, thanks. And if you think of anything, let me know. I'll leave you my cell number." I wrote it down on a napkin with confident efficiency, as if I gave my cell number out to strange men all the time.

Zeke gave me and Alex a back-and-forth look, like he was trying to figure out the situation. Then he pocketed the napkin, told me he'd call if he thought of anything, and left.

9

ALEX AND I FINISHED up our food—I'd gone for fries *again,* despite all my good intentions to lose the weight that had been creeping on all year—and stepped out onto the street. It was now after 8:00pm, and the twilight was deepening as Friday evening transitioned into Friday night, with all the promise of wildness that held.

"What do you think?" I asked Alex. "Keep checking bars, or follow up on this H woman? She's got to be the journalist, don't you think? Do you know anything more about her?"

"What if," he said, looking up and down the street instead of at me, "I dropped you off back home so you could follow up on H, while I started working Alvarado Street? I don't want you to mess up your knee on this mission."

I'd torn my left ACL during the spring. It was not healing well. I'd buckled down and had it looked at last month, shuddering with horror as I paid for an out-of-network provider. They'd prescribed physical therapy. I'd gone to a couple of sessions, and then stopped when I ran out of money. Plus, I'd felt even worse after the sessions than before them. I'd been assured that was normal and desirable. I had my doubts.

"Um," I said. "Okay. I guess. I'm not really sure what I'd be doing at home, though."

"Call Frank," he said. "Tell him what you found. Maybe he'll know something. I know he's been looking into the journalist on his down time already. If she does enough digging, we're all going to land in deep

33

shit. He's already engaging in major CYA. You should go back to HQ, see what you can find out, and wait for me or Frank—or Zeke—to call."

"Um," I said. "I guess that makes sense."

It was a little under fifteen minutes to get back to the apartment. I tried to probe Alex on the drive about the journalist, and, as delicately as I could, about what she might uncover that was so bad. Other than the obvious, that is. But he gave me monosyllabic answers and shrugs in response. I knew he was upset and under pressure and probably racked with guilt. I knew he was doing the best he could to be nice to me under the circumstances. But I still found his behavior annoying. And I didn't really know what to do next. Alex, Erin, and Frank were all the people with the real training and experience in intelligence gathering.

Not to mention the networks that would allow them to gather said intelligence. I felt helpless and out of my depth. I'd done my best on my own, and netted the interesting but so far useless information that Erin had had dinner on Wednesday with a woman whose name may or may not have begun with H, and that H had upset her. I guessed it was nice to know. But it wasn't exactly actionable. And I didn't see what else I could find out on my own, especially not stuck in the apartment. And the need to have someone there was nonexistent. We all had cell phones. I could answer the phone while bar-crawling with Alex just as well as I could sitting at his kitchen table.

Given his sour mood, I thought Alex was going to drop me off at the curb, but he parked the car and walked me inside. "Lock the door after me," he told me.

I gave him a sidewise look. "Are you, um...expecting *danger*?" I asked.

He shook his head. Too quickly. "This isn't a great neighborhood," he said. "You know that."

"Yeah, I do," I said. "And *you* know I always practice all reasonable safety protocols because of it. So what are you worried about? Is that why you want me to stay here instead of coming with you?"

He chewed on the left corner of his lower lip for a moment. I didn't think I'd ever seen him make such an anxious gesture before.

"It's messy," he finally said. "I mean, I don't know what the fuck Erin has gotten herself mixed up in, but it's really fucking messy, that I'm pretty damn sure of. And when she's drunk...she's...it's not pretty. I don't want you to have see that. And I'm afraid she might...I don't know...she might do some stuff that's not great. To you. I don't want you to have to deal with that. I don't want you to get dragged into all the bad shit that surrounds her. That surrounds *me*."

"You think she'd say hateful stuff to me?"

"Yeah. And...worse, maybe."

"You think she might *attack* me?"

He shrugged unhappily. "I don't want to think that...but she's really not herself when she's drunk. I'd rather you stayed far the fuck away from all that, Rowena."

"Do you think she's dangerous?" I asked. "To me, or to you, or to herself?"

He chewed on his lip some more. "I really don't want to think that. But I've got to, you know what I mean? I can't ignore the possibility that she might do something really stupid. She got a concealed carry permit this spring and she's been carrying a handgun in her purse..."

"Wait," I said. "You mean she just got a concealed carry permit this spring? Like, right before she was shot by Frank?"

Alex nodded. Miserably. "That's why they were at the range. She wanted to brush up on her firearms skills."

"*Why* did she get a concealed carry permit and a handgun?" I asked.

He made an I-don't-know gesture. "She didn't say. I didn't know anything about it until, you know, afterwards."

"But as far as you know, she still has the gun," I said. "She's potentially walking around right now, full of pain and maybe drunk off her ass, with a deadly weapon in her purse."

He nodded even more miserably.

"Okaaaayyy," I said. "Do you think we should call the police?"

He shook his head, a convulsive motion of denial. "That could bring even more shit down on her than she's already dealing with. If I could just find her before she does something stupid..."

"Okay," I said. "You go look for her. I'll call Frank. And I'll think about how else we might try to track her down."

10

ALEX LEFT, SLAMMING the sticky door behind him so hard that the dishes rattled on the shelves. The front—and only—door to his apartment didn't quite fit in the frame, so it required a good hard slam, and sometimes considerable shaking, jiggling, and prayers for mercy, to get it to shut enough to be able to shoot the deadbolt.

I shot the deadbolt. The door was still quivering in my hand. Alex must be really worked up.

I went over to the kitchen/dining room table and sat down. What was that noise? The dishes—all two plates and two bowls that Alex owned—were still rattling on their shelves. Jeez. This place was even more ramshackle than I'd thought.

My legs were quivering. What *was* this? I was tired, sure, but I didn't think I was *this* tired. Was I sick? What was that noise? Oh my God! Was I having aural hallucinations because I was having a stroke? No, wait. It was just a train...I wasn't in Indiana. There weren't any trains here...it must be a plane. We were right by Monterey Regional Airport. But planes didn't make the ground shake like this...not unless they were about to crash right into you.

I looked up at the ceiling in terror, as if I could see right through it to the plane plummeting straight at my head. The table was shaking under my hand. It must be just outside the house...it didn't *sound* like a plane.

The shaking and the deep rumbling I felt as much as heard stopped. I looked around in frantic confusion. Then I felt like an idiot. It had been an earthquake. Just an earthquake. The San Andreas fault ran through Monterey County, along with several smaller faults. By California standards, it wasn't a particularly active fault zone, and the chances of half the town cracking off and falling into the bay were apparently small. But minor quakes weren't uncommon. We'd already had one this summer. I just wasn't used to them, and hadn't thought this might be one. But it had to have been.

I brushed something off my face, then looked up again. Dust fell squarely into my eyes, sending me scurrying off to the bathroom to flush them out with cold water.

As I was bent over the sink, a soft paw reached out from behind the toilet and touched my ankle. I shrieked and jumped, spraying water everywhere. I don't know why. It was Fevronia, my tan long-haired rescue cat, whom I'd brought with me for the summer. Reaching out from hiding places and placing a paw on my ankle was one of her favorite hobbies. But it still made me leap like a gaffed salmon every time.

"I guess the earthquake didn't freak you out too much," I said, and reached down to pet her. Fevronia pinned back her ears, hissed at me, and darted off to the bedroom. At least she hadn't drawn blood.

When I came back into the dining room, I saw that a small crack had opened up where the wall met the ceiling. Dust and bits of plasterboard were drifting down onto the table.

What do I do? Is the whole place about to come down around my ears? I watched the crack for a couple of minutes. It didn't get any bigger, and after a while dust stopped floating down onto the table. We were probably safe enough. I'd point it out to Alex when he got back, and he'd probably notify the landlord, and the landlord would probably ignore it, and I'd be out of here by Sunday anyway and it wouldn't be my problem. Meanwhile, I couldn't use this as an excuse to get out of searching for Erin.

I wiped down the table. Then, unable to delay it any longer, I got out my phone and called Frank.

11

"HEY, ROWENA. YOU'RE early. You find something?"

Frank had answered on the first ring. I was going to have to start interacting with him, whether I wanted to or not.

"Maybe," I said. "What about you?"

"Nothing substantive yet."

I was impressed. I hadn't known Frank was capable of using words like "substantive." It was probably official-speak. He probably had an excellent command of that kind of professional lingo. It was the kind of thing I instinctively wanted to scoff at. But it made him sound more professional and less lecherous, so right now I was grateful.

"What you got?" he said. Not a hint of sexual innuendo. Maybe he wouldn't be so bad to work with. Maybe I was kidding myself.

I told him about Erin's dinner with H.

"I assume she's the journalist," I said. "Do you know anything more about her? Maybe she knows something."

"Yeah," said Frank. "Nice work." He sounded like he genuinely meant it. Good Lord. I was halfway to respecting him as a competent professional. Next thing I knew, I was going to start liking him.

"Unfortunately, I don't know a damn thing more than that," he said. "And I've been looking ever since Erin told me about her. I tried to get Erin to tell me, but for once she wouldn't open her fucking mouth. She's yak yak yak when she should shut up, and then silent as a fucking clam when she should talk."

My extremely lukewarm good feelings towards Frank started draining away again. Did he talk about Erin like this in front of her? I was pretty sure he did. *And* he'd shot her. In the breast. Maybe it was an accident, like they'd both claimed. Maybe it was one those accidentally-on-purpose things. In any case, she was still with him. Except, now she'd run away. Or disappeared, at least.

"I know she's been getting texts from her," Frank was saying. "'Cause she got one while we were together last weekend. Probably setting up the meeting on Wednesday. So this H woman's contact info is in her phone. If I had a court order, I might be able to access her text messages, depending on how she sent them. She uses regular texts when she messages me. Her cell service provider should have a record of those. But if she's using WhatsApp, they don't store those, so you have to have the actual phone itself to read them. I don't have her phone, and I don't have a court order to show to Verizon. No one's reported her missing, have they?"

"Not that I know of," I said.

"There's no waiting period to report a missing person in California," said Frank. "Miller could go ahead and file one right now. Only problem is, Erin's got a history of running off. No one's going to take this too seriously since she's done it a fucking million times before. And it's Friday night. The police'll have plenty of real work to do."

"Alex said she didn't normally miss work, though," I said.

"Yeah. That's what's got me worried. If she'd blown off our date tomorrow, I'd be like, whatever, she's just fucking around like she used to do to Miller all the damn time. I'd set her straight and move on. But her not showing up to work has got me worried. 'Specially with this journalist hounding her."

"Alex said she might have a gun," I said.

"Yeah. And normally I'd be like, whatever, about that too. It's not like she didn't carry a sidearm for years, right? But combined with blowing off work—that's bad."

"Yeah," I said.

"Tell you what," he said. "I'll go ahead and call Monterey PD, let them know what's going on. Maybe we can get things moving through official channels so they can ping her phone, maybe even get a court order for her phone records if we're lucky. Meanwhile, see what you can do to figure out who this H woman is."

"Um," I said. "How?"

"Well, Jesus Christ, you're the smartypants here. Figure it out."

"Um," I said. "Okay."

"Sorry," said Frank. "That was uncalled for. I'm just really worried about Erin."

"No problem," I said, too stunned by his apology to say anything else.

"And the rest of us," he went on. "We're looking at a whole world of shit coming down on our heads here, I don't have to tell you. The sooner we can find this fucking H, the better. So...who do you think would be doing that kind of a story? Miller said you used to date a journalist. Who does stories like that?"

"Investigative journalists," I said. "Either freelance, or for the big publications, like *The Washington Post.*"

"This sounds just like the kind of thing those fuckers at the *Post* would do."

"Um," I said. "Yeah. It does."

"So go look and see who covers stories like that."

"Um," I said. "That sounds like it could take a while. Especially since she could be working for dozens of publications, or freelancing, or..."

"I know." Frank cut me off before I could list all the reasons why this plan was a bad one. "I know it's a fucking long shot. But it's what we've got right now. You say Miller's doing leg work, going bar to bar?"

"Uh-huh."

"And I'll try going through the official channels. But like I said, you're the smartypants here. *And* you used to date a journalist. This is your area of expertise. Start looking around and see if you come up with something. If it pays off, great. If it doesn't, well, what else the fuck were you going to do tonight?"

"Great question," I said. "I'll take a look."

"Great," said Frank. "Get to it, then." He hung up before I could say anything else.

12

FRANK'S SUGGESTION seemed like an *extremely* long shot to me. Yes, doing an investigative piece on the US program of torture in Iraq was exactly the sort of thing *The Washington Post* would do. So would *The New York Times*, *The Atlantic*, *The New Yorker*, and probably a bunch of other publications. And according to Alex, she was working on a book, which meant she could be doing all this as a freelancer. But I didn't have anything else to go on, so I might as well keep myself busy while I waited for Alex to come back.

I scrolled through the "Meet the Investigative Team" page on *The Washington Post's* website. No one remotely fit the description of the woman we were looking for. I checked out the "Our People" page on *The New York Times's* website. Absolutely zip. I spent a while scrolling through the Wikipedia page on *NYT* employees. There were only two people whose first names began with H. Both of them were men, and one of them was dead.

Hmm. This line of inquiry was looking pretty fruitless. I started a Google search on the US program of torture in Iraq, in case she'd already published something on it. I got 5,330,000 hits. The first five pages had nothing written by a woman with a first name beginning with H. Going through the other pages would take such a ridiculously long time it wasn't even worth thinking about.

Think! I told myself. *That's what you're good at!* Although I hated to admit it, Frank's designation of me as the "smartypants" of the group was weirdly flattering. Oddly, considering that I had a PhD in an esoteric and difficult subject, I had never thought of myself as that smart. My childhood patchwork of Montessori schools, Waldorf schools, and homeschooling meant that I'd never gotten grades or class rankings the way kids who went to regular schools did, which meant that I'd never spent a lot of time fretting about my comparative intelligence or lack thereof. I was just however smart I was, and that was fine.

I'd done well in college, but academic achievement had never been my prime motivator. Living in Russia and working with refugees and torture victims had hammered home to me how weak my Russian skills were and how limited my life experience was. Of course, that job had also expanded my Russian skills and my life experience until they were both well beyond that of my peers, but the basic attitude it had instilled in me was one of humility. Doing a PhD had made me realize how unacademic I was compared to most of the other students in the program, and since the program had been at Indiana University, a state school in the Midwest, I had learned quick enough to feel inferior to the students from the Ivy League and big West Coast schools.

All this meant that I wasn't used to thinking of myself as the "smart one" in a group. I was the nice one, the reliable one, the one who met deadlines and did the paperwork and organized events and showed up when no one else would. My advisor had made occasional comments about how high the faculty's expectations were for me, but that still seemed part and parcel with my reliability, not a sign of my brilliance. The other people, the ones who couldn't make their deadlines or show up to their events on time or make sure their documents were in order, were the smart ones. I was just their sidekick, smoothing the bumps in the road and oiling the machinery behind the scenes.

And that was the position I thought I'd been placed in again here. I'd provided moral support for Alex on the drive up to Erin's place and back, and asked the questions at the restaurant when he couldn't, and then allowed myself to be sent home when he decided it would be easier to operate without me.

It wasn't that I thought of myself as weak, or stupid, or useless, or passive, or submissive, or anything like that. In fact, I thought of myself as a competent, take-charge kind of person. I just didn't think of myself as *special*. I mean, I knew I was special and unique in the way that everyone is special and unique, but I didn't think of myself as the person to come up with the brilliant solution that would save the day. Especially in a situation like this. Surely this was a situation where Frank and Alex would do all the real work, and I'd be supportive and make cups of tea or something.

I had the sudden sickening thought that that's what I'd done all along for Dima as well. He'd been the one who *mattered*. I'd just been playing a supporting role. And while we all played supporting roles in the lives of those around us, I'd been playing a supporting role in my own life as well. I'd made it all about *him* and *his* career and *his* needs. And then he'd sent me away, and I'd had nothing left to live for. My lightning-strike love had left me charred and shattered, and I had never been able to pick up the pieces.

I knew that wasn't really true. I'd finished my degree and begun my career and worked on my research and started a new relationship and done all sorts of things that should have been meaningful and fulfilling. But in my heart of hearts, I didn't think any of those things were that important. Because, compared with what Dima had been doing, they *weren't*. They didn't give me the thing I needed most in the world: a deep sense of purpose. My job was just that: a job, and one that involved a lot of busywork and abuse and not a lot of money or security. And I didn't even have the flimsy excuse of needing to support my family.

My research should have been important and meaningful, but like most academic research done these days, it was mainly about pleasing the right people and ticking the right boxes. The world would probably be a better place if I didn't do it. My teaching *was* important, of that

I was certain, but I was still pretty interchangeable. No university, and few students, would care about *me* as a person at all. I was just a service for them, one that could be switched out as needed with no real change in the quantity or quality of the content produced.

Get a grip! I told myself. *Now is not the time! Besides, you've just had a brilliant idea.* All this melancholy musing about the meaninglessness of my life and my pointless devotion to another person had, in fact, opened up a useful avenue of investigation.

I pulled up WhatsApp on my phone and started a message thread to Dima.

13

I HAVE A QUESTION, I wrote. *It's fairly urgent. Do you know a female journalist, probably American, first name starts with H? She probably covers conflict, or human rights, or something like that. Maybe about 50? Fluffy hair with gray streaks?*

There was a ten-hour time difference between Ukraine and California. It was already the next morning where Dima was. Of course, that didn't mean he'd be available. I should get back to trawling through the internet in case I got lucky and stumbled upon H on my own.

After another half hour of that, I was no closer to discovering her identity or Erin's whereabouts. I was debating texting Alex to see if he'd made any progress, when my phone *pinged.*

I checked my notifications. Alex. I hated myself for feeling a tiny bit disappointed when I saw his name on the screen.

May have gotten a lead, he wrote. *The bouncer at the third bar I went to remembers Erin coming in Thursday night. She's a regular there, so he's pretty sure.*

That's great! I wrote back. *Does he know anything else?*

Just that she came alone, sat in the corner by herself, had a couple of drinks while texting up a storm, then left about 10pm.

Did he see which way she went?

Nope. It's not much of a lead. But it's better than nothing. At least we know she was alive and in town then. And it also sounds like she was pretty stressed about something. I'm going to keep going, see if I can find out anything more.

Sounds good, I wrote. *Meanwhile, I'll keep working here. Frank suggested I try to look for the journalist.*

Do you think you have any chance of finding her? I could feel Alex's skepticism coming over the text. It was well founded.

A very slim one. But I can't think of anything better to do. If you have any suggestions, let me know!

No, he texted. *If I think of anything, I'll let you know, but for now, that seems as good as anything else. All right, I'm off to the next seedy dive bar. Wish me luck!*

Luck! I wrote back.

I checked the time. 9:47. I really wanted to start getting ready for bed. But even if I wanted to sleep while the others were out searching for Erin, I didn't think I'd be able to manage it. Guess I'd better keep working, then.

I began a search of local papers, starting with the *Monterey Herald* and expanding out from there. Maybe this H person was a local journalist and was targeting Erin because she was nearby.

I'd gotten as far as the *San Francisco Chronicle* with no results when my phone *pinged.* I picked it up, expecting it to be Alex again, or maybe Frank.

Darling Inna, the message read. *Do you maybe mean Heather Ramirez?*

14

VERY POSSIBLY, I wrote back. *Do you know her?*

Not very well. She spent a couple of weeks here in Donetsk last winter. Then she left to go to Syria. But I think she's only sort of a war correspondent. She's interested in corruption in the military and the government. I think she's writing a book on torture, which is why I thought of her.

That could be her! Do you have her contact information? It's important. And urgent.

I don't. But my friend Dave Wilkinson might. Let me ask him and get back to you.

Thanks!!!!

Of course. It's my pleasure to help you. I'll be in touch soon.

I spent longer than I should have staring at that last text. What did "it's my pleasure to help you" mean? Aside from the obvious. But why had he said it? Dima was not normally a very effusive person, unless he was letting the world know what he thought about crime, corruption, and incompetence. Then he was astonishingly eloquent. But other than that, he didn't express his feelings much. And that was such a...*something* kind of thing to say. It was the kind of thing you'd say to a prospective lover to show them you were interested, that's what it was.

I chewed on my lower lip a little. How long would I have to wait to hear from him again? However long it took him to get in touch with this Dave Wilkinson person, who I thought was another journalist. Who knows how long that would be. Meanwhile, though, I could start searching for Heather Ramirez on my own.

I typed "Heather Ramirez" into the search bar, and got 16,700,000 hits. Well, that would take a while to go through. I added "investigative journalist" to the search. That narrowed it down to 761,000 hits. But the second hit on the first page was for a website for a freelance journalist. When I brought up the site, there was a photograph on the home page. It was a flattering professional headshot, but it was still of a hard-bitten, slightly overweight woman who had never been pretty and now that she was approaching fifty had given up on personal appearance almost entirely, with a face that had seen a lot of harsh weather and harsher sights, and big poofy hair in a mullet-ish 80s throwback style.

I might have found our journalist, I texted Frank and Alex, and sent them the link to Heather Ramirez's website.

15

GREAT JOB! Frank texted back. *See if you can get in touch with her.*

That surprised me. Somehow I'd assumed that he or Alex would the ones to talk to Heather. This was their search; I was just doing the computer stuff. But here Frank was telling me to get in touch with Heather, and Alex hadn't responded at all.

Will do, I replied. Then I started going through the site looking for contact info.

Unfortunately, there wasn't a phone number that I could find. There was an "About" page with Heather's background and education. There was a page on past projects with links to some of her more prominent articles. There was a page on current projects, which I read with interest. She was indeed working on a book about torture by the US military, which had already been picked up by a major publisher. And there was a contact form that I could fill out if I wanted to get in touch with her.

I went ahead and filled it out, explaining that I was a friend of Erin's, that she was missing, and that I was concerned that either she or Heather could be in danger, and to please contact me ASAP. I spent a moment worrying about telling a stranger and a journalist something that sensitive and potentially explosive, but I wanted a quick response, and this seemed the best way to get it.

Besides, unlike Alex and Frank, I was naturally disposed to like and trust Heather. I did in fact believe it likely that she had our best interests at heart. Well, not theirs, perhaps, but the nation's as a whole, yes. I knew all too well how relentless journalists could be in pursuing a story, and how willing they could be to sacrifice other things, but I still thought that Heather might be our best chance at actually finding and helping Erin. And if not, then maybe she would feel some pangs of conscience about putting pressure on an emotionally fragile person, which would enable her to achieve some worthwhile personal growth.

I added my email and phone number and hit "Send." Then I texted Frank and Alex to let them know I'd done it.

Great! Frank wrote back. *I've been on the phone with Monterey PD. They said they haven't seen any sign of Erin, but they'll keep an eye out for her, see if they can locate her by pinging her phone. Although they might not tell me if they find her. They seem to think I'm a dangerous ex-boyfriend who needs to be kept away :) :) And I talked to her parents. They haven't heard anything from her for months. No surprises there, lol. Too busy being rich San Diego socialites to pay attention to their only daughter. Anything to report, Miller?*

Nothing, Alex texted. *I'm just stepping out of my sixth seedy bar for the evening. So far I've only had the one hit. There are a couple more places to try, and then I'm out of ideas.*

I think Rowena's on our best line of inquiry right now anyway, Frank wrote. *Any word from her yet, Ro?*

I had never told Frank he could call me Ro. I had never told *Alex* he could call me Ro. The only person permitted to call me Ro was my brother John. But here Frank was, doing it anyway on his own initiative. I thought for a nanosecond about making a fuss about it. Then I decided it would cause me a lot of trouble and fuss, and also make me look weak. One of the many useful life lessons I'd learned from speaking a foreign language and spending a lot of time in foreign countries is that fretting over what people call you is often a big waste of time and energy. The more you do it, the more power you give them over you.

No, I wrote back. *But I only emailed her five minutes ago. It might take a little while. And I'm waiting to hear if I can get her cell number, but I don't have it yet.*

Good going, texted Frank. *How'd you get this intel, anyway? I'm impressed!*

Personal contact, I wrote. *I have an in with the journalism world, remember? I asked around and got her name as possibly our person. And I'm waiting to hear back from a friend of a friend about her cell number. Her website says she lives in Salinas. I'm doing a search in the local White Pages right now to see if I can get her phone number that way. Oops, looks like I have to pay to get that info.*

I'll do it, Frank texted. *Meanwhile, stand by for any emails from her.*

Will do, I promised, and went back to hovering by the computer.

16

AFTER HALF AN HOUR I still hadn't heard anything from Heather. I'd spent the time skimming through the website for the clinical trial Dima had asked me to look into. As far as I could tell, it looked legit. I texted him to tell him that, and got no response. Dima wasn't always big on responding.

At 10:30 Frank texted to say that he'd gotten Heather's number and called it, but only reached her voicemail. He'd left a message to call him back as soon as she could. So far he'd heard nothing.

Could mean she's out on a hot date, he wrote. *Could mean she's avoiding us, or in trouble. Or could mean she has another phone she's using for some reason. I'm going to give Salinas PD a call just to give them a head's up. I'll let you know if I hear anything.*

I'm done here, Alex texted. *No one knows anything. Heading home.*

Copy that. Stand by for further instructions. Over and out.

I resisted an eye roll. Probably that was not an affectation. Probably that was the most natural way for Frank to communicate.

I shut down my computer and got up to get a drink of water. My hair fell in my face. My hair was in serious need of cutting. One of the many things I hadn't had the time or the money to do all summer. What little time, money, and energy I'd had to spare for self-care had gone into my knee.

Grit fell out of my hair and down my face. Ugh. I'd been sitting here all evening with ceiling dirt in my hair. I headed for the shower.

When I got out, Alex was just coming through the door. He looked exhausted, and somehow sad and lifeless in a way I'd never seen in him before.

"Hey," I said. "You look beat. Maybe we should call it a night."

"Yeah." He stood in the center of the tiny kitchen, looking lost. "I guess. I just feel like I'm letting Erin down if I'm not searching for her, you know what I mean?"

"I know," I said. "But you've done what you can. We've all done what we can. There's a good chance we'll find her soon. And ultimately, Erin's a grown woman who's made her own choices."

He flinched. "You think something bad's happened to her?"

"I hope not. I think it's a good sign that the police don't know anything. If she'd driven off a bridge or something, they'd know. She's probably hiding out somewhere, feeling like shit. And that's sad, and I hope we can find her and help her. But she made her choices. She made her bed, and none of us can lie in it for her."

Alex flinched again. "It's not her fault," he said.

"No. Not entirely. I know you said she had a rough childhood..."

"Yeah. A real poor little Southern California rich girl. What was it Pearl Jam said? That's how it was for Erin. Her dad never paid her any attention, and she wasn't something pretty for her mom to wear. So she started chasing after boys to get any semblance of attention and affection." He shook himself. "I'm pretty sure something...awful happened to her in high school. Like, really awful. I'm sure you get the picture."

"Yeah," I said. "I do. Poor girl."

"Yeah. So she joined up, maybe to piss off her parents, maybe to impress a guy, maybe to prove she was tough and macho and not a victim. And she wasn't. As long as she was wearing that uniform, she was the opposite."

"Sort of," I said. "Sounds like she was still a victim, in a way. She was used by others to carry out their terrible agenda, and now she's paying the price for it."

"Yeah. Yeah. Exactly. I guess you could say that in a way, her superior officers did to her just what those high school boys did—or worse. They treated her as a thing to be used for their purposes and thrown away to face the consequences. But at least she got to get a little taste of power in the process. Not that it did her any good. Probably it just did her more harm."

"Power often does," I said.

"Yeah. And in her case...you know, she's not a bad person. Not at heart." Alex raised his eyes to mine. Tears were standing in them. Jealousy lanced through me at the realization that the only time I'd ever seen him cry was over Erin. Guilt went chasing right after it.

"I'm sure she's not a bad person," I said. In fact, I thought she *was* a bad person, or at least a person who was so consumed by her own misery that she made everyone around her miserable too. I was aware that my perspective was not completely objective.

"And," Alex was saying, looking at the sink, which was dripping slightly, rather than at me, "it's like she's never had the chance to grow up. Not really. Neither of us did. We've been completely infantilized. Her especially, but me too. We've never been allowed to grow up and learn how to be decent human beings."

"I know," I said. "Believe me, I know all about being infantilized. I'm in academia, remember?"

He smiled. Bitterly. At the dripping sink, not at me. "Yeah," he said. "I know, right? I've spent my whole adult life knuckling under to infantilizing professions. First I was in college, and then I was in the military, and then I was back in college. Even when I got my PhD and started working as a professor, I was still stuck in a totally infantile state. Because even though both the military and higher ed will tell you that they're all about making a man or a free-thinking intellectual or a whatever of you, and they even try, okay, pathetically, but they try, to do so, at their heart they're completely infantilizing.

"Higher ed is supposed to teach you to think for yourself, but for fuck's sake, I wasn't even allowed to make a ten-point vocab quiz without supervision. I remember standing there by the copy machine and printing off the quizzes I had been forced to redo because the language teaching director decided we hadn't picked the right vocab words from the vocab list of the first chapter of our first-year textbook, and thinking, 'I'm thirty-three years old, I graduated summa cum laude from one of the most prestigious universities in the nation, I'm fucking *war veteran*, for Christ's sake, and they won't even let me do basic clerical work without constant supervision and critique.

"And the military wasn't much better. Okay, so we were responsible for expensive equipment. We were even responsible for making life-and-death decisions. But the basic mindset was one of such extreme abdication of responsibility that no one really thought at all. Everyone was always looking to the person above them to tell them what to do, say, even think. I could feel myself regressing to babyhood by the second. Except that even as a baby I'm pretty sure I thought more for myself."

"Very likely," I said.

"And it was ten times worse for Erin. Because she was a girl, and because she was herself. There was something about her that made people want to take advantage of her. At least that's what it seemed like to me."

"It seems like it to me too," I said. "Unfortunately. Maybe we can help her, I don't know, learn how not to be victimized." *Ugh! Why did I say that! I don't **want** to help her! Talk about letting yourself be victimized!* But that wasn't quite true. Okay, it was true that I didn't want to help her. But that didn't mean I shouldn't. Despite what a lot of American self-help gurus seemed to think, abandoning people when they really needed you was not a sign of strength. Erin did, in fact, need my help, so I should give it to her. It was as simple as that.

"Let's go to bed," I said.

Alex gave me a surprised look.

"We've done all we can do tonight," I told him. "We've set all the wheels that we can in motion. Staying up all night wearing ourselves out won't do anything for Erin, and it might mean we won't be able to help her when she needs us. We should rest in order to be ready for tomorrow."

"Yeah," said Alex. "I guess."

"But take a shower first," I told him. "You smell like a dozen dive bars."

He almost smiled. "Okay," he said. "You're right."

17

I WOKE UP EVERY 90 minutes like clockwork. Probably because of REM cycles or something. Every time, I checked my phone. Absolutely nothing.

Alex slept even more poorly than I did. In fact, I wasn't sure he slept at all. But by 6:00am he had drifted off into something that resembled sleep. I lay perfectly still, staring at the ceiling and trying not to wake him.

At 6:13 my phone, which I'd had by my pillow, despite my fear of it giving me brain cancer, vibrated.

Moving with the care of someone juggling fine china in a hurricane, I picked up my phone and brought it to my face.

Darling Inna! Good news. Dave got in touch with Heather. She said she'll talk to you. Here's her cell phone number.

Thanks!! I texted back. *I'm in your debt!*

You could never be in my debt, Inna. Good luck! Let me know how it goes.

I squinted my sleep-blurred eyes at that text. Was I reading it right? Had Dima actually said that? What the *fuck* was he up to?

Maybe he's not "up to" anything, I told myself. *Maybe he's just being nice, and you're reading **way** too much into it.*

I told myself to stop thinking about it and worry about what to do with Heather's number instead. Call her right away? It was 6:15 on Saturday morning. Most people would not be happy to receive a call at that time. On the other hand, why had Dima only gotten back to me now? Presumably because he'd only just gotten her number, which meant she had only just given it to Dave...unless there'd been a delay somewhere in the relay process...

Wait until 7:00, I counseled myself. *Try and get some more sleep.*

I put down my phone, closed my eyes, and tried to think sleep-inducing thoughts. It only made me more restless.

At 6:27 I gave up, got out my phone again, and sent a quick text message to Heather. If she was asleep, I reasoned, she'd have her ringer off and I wouldn't be disturbing her. If she was awake, then she could answer. But she was almost certainly asleep.

At 6:29 a reply popped up on my phone screen.

Everyone must be really desperate to find Erin. You messaged me yesterday evening, I had some FBI agent leaving me messages last night, and now you're texting me again. Dave says you're okay, so I'll answer your questions if I can. Fire away.

Wow, you're up early! I texted back.

So are you. What do you want to know?

When was the last time you saw Erin?

Wednesday, she wrote back promptly. *We had dinner together at Duffy's. But she didn't want to talk to me, so I left. What's up with her? She's run off, you say?*

Yes. We're trying to find her. Do you have any suggestions?

Aren't you her friend?

Yes. It seemed best to keep it simple. *But maybe she said something to you that would point us in the right direction.*

I don't know what to tell you. She told me to go to hell on Wednesday, and I haven't heard from her since.

What were you talking about that got her so upset? I asked. Maybe it would be helpful. Probably it wouldn't, but it would ease my curiosity to know.

That's between her and me.

Fair enough, I wrote. *I think I can guess anyway. I'm just wondering what it was about that last time that set her off. You'd been talking to her for weeks, right?*

Right, she confirmed. *But this time—oh, fuck, might as well tell you—this time I showed her some testimony from one of the men she'd "interrogated." About what it was like for him, and what his life has been like since then. And she got upset and started telling me I didn't know what it was like, what *he* was like, the situation they all found themselves in. So I said, "Well, tell me then." That's when she had her meltdown.*

Not surprising, I wrote back.

No, but interesting. I'd really love to get her side of the story, especially since otherwise, she's going to look like the black-hat villain of the piece. But I know she's not. Or her hat was far from the blackest. I'm sure she could name some names, blow this whole thing wide open, if only she'd work up the nerve to do it. But as it stands, she's going to be my main bad guy unless she gives me something else to work with.

Does she know that? I asked.

Yeah. My guess is that's why she's so messed up about it.

Yeah, I wrote. *Look, let me know if you hear from her, okay? We really are worried about her. And look out for yourself, okay? I don't want to think that she's dangerous, but, well, you're in a dangerous business.*

Yeah, she texted. *Dave said you used to be Dima Kuznetsov's girlfriend?*

That's right.

*That's the only reason I agreed to talk to you. *Major* respect to him for what he does. Although he was probably a pretty shitty boyfriend, I'm guessing :) :)*

Something like that, I wrote.

LOL, no kidding. I've dated men like him. Good God. I'm no angel myself, but Jesus Christ. I'm better off on my own, I figured that out years ago. Anyway, it sounds like you're a pretty cool person too, so I'll give you a heads-up if I hear from Erin. You do the same, okay?

Okay, I wrote. *And for what it's worth, I think you're doing the right thing. If I can convince her to talk to you, I will—although I don't have much pull with her.*

Still appreciate it :) :) Good luck!

Thanks.

I put down my phone. Alex had opened his eyes at some point during this and was now on his side, looking at me with a tired but intent gaze.

"That looked important," he said.

"It was. Sort of." I outlined the conversation I'd just had with Heather.

"Damn," he said when I'd finished. "I'd been hoping that we'd track down Heather and she'd lead us directly to Erin. But we're no closer to finding her than we were before."

"Yeah," I said. "Still good to know, though. What next?"

He gave a sort of half-groan and flopped onto his back. "We talk to Frank," he said, speaking to the ceiling. "And we try to figure out where we go from here."

18

I TEXTED FRANK ABOUT the new developments while Alex was in the shower.

Good work, he texted back. *Although I'm pissed as shit at this Heather chick for blowing me off and talking to you :) :) How'd you get her to open up, anyway?*

Personal connections, I wrote.

No shit? What kind of personal connections you got that could crack a tough cookie like that?

My ex-fiancé has a lot of cachet with other journalists. She agreed to talk to me for his sake.

Well damn :) :) We'd better keep you around :) :) You still in touch with him?

I stared at the phone. What business was it of Frank's? Why on earth was he asking? Other than the obvious, of course: he was a nosy asshole.

That's how I got her number, I wrote. *I asked him, and he asked her.*

Good for you, babe! Work those personal contacts! I know it hurts to ask an ex for favors, but sometimes you gotta suck it up and do what's best for the mission. And if there's still something between you, you can work that too. I bet he's still hot for you, huh?

I stared at the phone a bit more. Ugh. How did I respond to that?

I'm glad I could help, I texted.

Let's get together for breakfast and strategy, he wrote. *I'm here in Salinas, at Erin's place. No sign of her all night. Why don't I drive down, meet you in Monterey, since that's the last place she was seen, and we put our heads together?*

Okay.

08:00, Tidal Coffee.

See you there, I wrote.

Alex came out of the shower. "What's up?" he asked.

"War council with Frank at eight," I told him.

He nodded. "Makes sense. Frank knows what he's doing."

I opened my mouth to point out that Alex had told me on multiple occasions how much he hated Frank. And he'd been beside himself over the shooting this spring. He'd wanted to cut off all contact with him, and spent several weeks trying to convince Erin to do the same. But she hadn't listened, and now Alex seemed to be coming around to a pro-Frank point of view.

Worse than that, I was starting to feel a tiny pro-Frank sprout unfurling inside of me as well. A big part of it was probably just proximity. If you spent enough time with someone, oxytocin would do its thing, and you'd bond with them whether you liked them or not. And I was developing a certain grudging respect for Frank's intelligence, even if it did seem largely to manifest itself as low animal cunning.

He SHOT Erin! I reminded myself. *In the breast!* As an armchair psychologist, I found that particular detail significant. Maybe it was an accident. Maybe he even consciously believed it was an accident. But he'd still aimed a loaded gun at her left breast and pulled the trigger, whether he consciously intended to or not.

"You need to take a shower?" Alex asked, breaking me out of my Frank-inspired reverie on the workings of the human subconscious.

I shook my head. "I took one after the earthquake dumped a bunch of dust and dirt on me last night. I'm good to go."

"Oh shit, right, the earthquake. I'd better text the building manager and let her know what's going on with that." He checked his phone. "I can do it on the way. Come on, let's go."

19

AFTER A SHORT ARGUMENT, Alex allowed me to drive my car, so that he could do the texting he needed to on the way over.

"You see?" I said as I turned onto Del Monte Avenue. "The car's working just fine."

A nasty grinding noise emitted from the gearbox as I shifted into second. Alex looked up from his phone, his face wry.

"Okay, okay, I brought that on myself. I should have known better than to brag about how well it's doing."

"Yeah, Jesus, Rowena, what's wrong with you?"

The words weren't kind. But his smile was warm and teasing. For a moment I could feel that connection between us that had been there from the first day we'd met at that awful faculty meeting, when he'd trembled every time we'd leaned in close to each other. That connection had only grown stronger as we'd worked together, and then even stronger, strangely, when we'd been apart. That had been part of what had convinced me that we had a chance, we had a future together.

But now that we'd spent the summer actually living together, it felt like the connection was fraying. And it wasn't because we fought over how to hang up the towels or who was going to do the dirty dishes. We didn't. It was because...because...dammit, I didn't *know* what was damaging the invisible cord that tied us together.

You DO know! I told myself. *It's the cords tying you to others. They're pulling the two of you apart.*

I didn't like that thought at all. Lots of people had exes, and still managed to make lives, *good* lives, together with someone. But maybe the issue here was that the exes weren't so ex as they should be.

Then you have to work harder at it! I told myself. *You have to* **choose** *each other, forsaking all others and all that stuff.*

But when I put it like that to myself, I wasn't sure I was ready.

"Building manager said she'll come by this morning and check out the damage," Alex announced, looking up from his phone again. "She doesn't think it's serious, but she's going to take a look at it anyway. She said a couple other tenants have reported cracks in the walls and ceilings too."

"Wow," I said. "What can they do about it?"

"Realistically?" He shrugged. "Not much. Not unless they think there's been structural damage."

"Jeez," I said. "California is scary."

"Scarier than hurricanes?"

"We don't get a lot of hurricanes in my part of Georgia," I pointed out.

"No, just blistering, soul-searing heat. And bugs. And fucking poisonous snakes as long as your arm."

"Hardly anyone ever *dies* from any of that, though," I said. "Cottonmouths are unlikely to go after you as long as you stay on dry land."

"So you say. I'm pretty sure my soul starts leaving my body at the very thought."

"Yankee," I said.

"You better believe it—looks like Frank's here already."

I pulled into the Cannery Row parking lot, where Frank was just getting out of his car. His back was to us, but that red buzz cut going to gray and that physique of a vigorous clan chieftain in the Highlands was unmistakable.

He turned and saw us as I was pulling into a spot two spaces over. "You folks are here early," he said, coming over to us. It was 7:50.

"So are you," I pointed out.

He shrugged. "Couldn't sleep. Couldn't sit around her empty house doing nothing. I wanted to get started. So here I am." He rubbed his eyes. Up close, he looked even more like a Highland chieftain, with ruddy skin that had seen too much sun, and a muscled body that still looked strong and vigorous, despite the beginnings of middle-aged spread. When he smiled, like he was doing right now, the animal magnetism flowed out and caught anyone in its path. Including, to my intense annoyance, me. I didn't like Frank. I didn't even think he was good-looking in any conventional sense. But wherever he went, heads turned, and people jumped to do his bidding.

While we walked over he filled us in on his side of the search. He'd driven over to her house in Salinas late in the evening and spent the night there. There'd been no sign of her.

"The Monterey PD called right before I left this morning and told me they had reason to believe she was safe, but they wouldn't tell me where the fuck she is. They must have pinged her phone and found her, but they're convinced I'm a fucking abusive boyfriend she's on the run from," he told us. He rubbed his face again, sounding more distracted than angry about it. "But I went through her bathroom and closet. Her travel bag's gone, along with a couple of her favorite outfits and her makeup and hair things."

"That's good, right?" I said. "It means she wasn't, I don't know, kidnapped or something. Or that she was planning to...harm herself."

"Yeah. But...I dunno," he said. "Something about it isn't right. When she's all fucked up and in a bad headspace, she doesn't pack an overnight back and bring her hairdryer and her lip gloss collection. She just disappears and then comes back the next day looking like something the cat drug in. But this time she had a plan. But if she had a plan, why'd she cut out of work without telling anyone? Not to mention that fucking barbecue we're supposed to go to. I already called my friends up and said we wouldn't be able to make it. And I'm pretty fucking pissed about that for your sake, Ro. I really wanted you to meet these people, get to know 'em, make the good impression on 'em I know you could. But she's fucked things up for you too, as well as me and Miller. Only this time it looks like a premeditated fuck-up."

"Yeah," I said.

We went in, ordered, and sat down. Frank started going over the possibilities again.

"Whaddya think, Ro?" he asked me. "Is this Heather chick telling the truth? Maybe she was winding you up, and she and Erin had really made plans to get together so that Erin could spill everything, and she was just telling you she didn't know where Erin was."

"I don't *think* she was lying," I said. "But I don't know her, and we were texting. It's entirely possible that I'm wrong. But why would she lie?"

Frank shrugged. "Who the fuck knows? 'Cause she likes fucking with us? 'Cause she's afraid of us? 'Cause she and Erin have cooked up some million-dollar scheme they don't want to cut us in on?"

"Why would she be afraid of us?" I asked. "What kind of million-dollar scheme could she and Erin have cooked up?"

Frank and Alex exchanged glances. For a moment I could see a connection between them, a cord tying them together even more tightly than the one that tied me and Alex together. Alex had told me back in the spring that he didn't think Frank remembered him from their time in Iraq together. Alex had been a minor desk jockey, a low-level bureaucrat who'd processed the voluminous paperwork that a state-sponsored program of torture and interrogation generated. Or so he said. I'd never doubted him before. But now, seeing that look between him and Frank, I found myself wondering. It was clear that even if Frank hadn't remembered him before, he did now, and that they both knew more than they were telling me.

"See, Ro," said Frank after a long silence, "Erin, well...she knows stuff."

"Yeah," I said. "I gathered."

"And not just ordinary stuff you'd expect her to know. Like, about...all that. Other stuff."

"Stuff worth a million dollars?" I asked.

Frank and Alex both nodded tightly.

"Um," I said. "Okay. Is this something I want to know about too?"

They both shook their heads.

"*Should* I know about it?" I pressed. "Am I in danger because of it?"

Alex shook his head in immediate and vehement denial. Frank paused.

"I don't wanna think so, Ro," he said. He paused again, in obvious thought. "Nah," he said. "You shouldn't be in any danger because of it. As long as you don't get mixed up in it too much. Don't get in anyone's way."

"Um," I said. "Okay. How do I make sure I don't get in anyone's way?"

Frank and Alex shared another look. I hated it even more than the previous look. It spoke so strongly of shared experience, shared knowledge, shared complicity in something I could never share with them.

"Maybe you should go back to the apartment," Alex said. "Spend the day there."

"Like, you mean, in *hiding?*"

He winced. "No, just...keeping a low profile."

I wanted to protest. I wanted to demand what on earth was going on. I wanted to point out that all the breaks in the case we'd gotten so far had been because of me and my effort and my personal contacts. Then I thought of all the secrets they were keeping from me, and my extreme lack of desire to get mixed up in whatever dirty business they were involved in, that had fucked Erin up so much she had spent the past decade barely functional, that was eating at Alex's soul and making him betray the good man he should have been.

"Okay," I said. "Good idea. I need to do laundry and pack and stuff anyway. I'll go home and do that. Let me know if you need me to do any more computer searches or anything like that. And I'll let you know if I hear from Heather or Erin."

Both men relaxed. "Great," said Alex. "That's great. Great plan." He smiled, rebuilding for a moment that connection that had always been between us. "Thanks, Rowena. You're really helping us out."

"No problem," I said.

20

ALEX AND FRANK DECIDED to take Frank's car back to Salinas. The plan was for them to do a thorough search of Erin's house and see if they found anything useful.

"It's going to be really embarrassing for everyone if it turns out she was taking a long weekend at a spa and just forgot to tell you," I said. I knew that wasn't super likely, since it seemed like no one at work had known about it, but maybe she *had* told the necessary admin people, and just forgotten to tell Alex—or more likely, deliberately avoided telling him. Maybe she was feeling completely overwhelmed by everything and had decided to spend three days on her own, getting massages and mud treatments and thinking about what to do about her current boyfriend who'd shot her (in the breast!), her ex-boyfriend she couldn't seem to let go of, and the ugly mess that was threatening to come pouring down on her head. The fact that she'd packed seemed like a very good sign to me.

"Nah," said Frank. "She's fucked up so many times she's gotta know this is what you get."

"Oh," I said. "Okay. Well, good luck." And I headed back to the apartment.

I really did need to do laundry, so the first thing I did was take a load into the rather grim little laundry room off to the side of the apartment building. It had a small crack at the top of the wall that I hadn't noticed there before, presumably from yesterday's earthquake. But the rust-spotted washer still worked as well as it ever had.

I left my clothes chugging away and went back up to the apartment. After a moment of trying to convince myself that I should really do some cleaning, I pulled out my laptop instead and started searching.

The first thing I looked up was Heather Ramirez's articles for the past couple of years. She had been published an average of once a month in that time, in a lot of the major publications you'd expect to feature a serious investigative reporter.

I skimmed through the articles. A lot of stuff about Syria, the Oil-for-Food program, the Gaza Strip, the Oil-for-Food program, the Donbass, the Oil-for-Food program...that was weird. The Oil-for-Food program, in which Iraq had been allowed to sell oil in exchange for food and medicine, had been phased out years ago. Why was Heather writing about it now?

I read the articles through carefully. I had only the vaguest memories of the Oil-for-Food program from when it was actually running, so most of this was news to me.

It had, I learned, been started in 1995 as a way to try to corral the Saddam Hussein regime while also providing the Iraqi people with desperately needed humanitarian supplies—and, of course, let the rich countries get their hands on that sweet, sweet Iraqi oil. That part was not in the official program description, but Heather and I both thought it was a major factor.

It had been de facto ended in 2003, with the US invasion of Iraq. Subsequent investigations had discovered widespread corruption, with foreign contractors providing kickbacks to highly placed officials in the Iraqi government, and ordinary Iraqi citizens receiving expired or spoiled food and medication.

There was nothing surprising about that, although the $10 billion in illegal money that had been pocketed was pretty impressive. But bribes and kickbacks were how a lot of regimes worked. Without them, the gears of government would grind to a halt, and nothing would get done at all.

There was also nothing surprising in Russia being the number one foreign beneficiary. The USSR and then Russia had maintained close ties with various Middle Eastern regimes for decades, and corruption was the default method of doing business. And as Heather pointed out, the program had in fact achieved its main aim, preventing the Saddam Hussein regime from creating weapons of mass destruction. $10 billion in kickbacks might be an acceptable price for that. Too bad about the lengthy and destructive war we'd engaged in to find that out.

More surprising were the allegations that Kofi Annan, then Secretary-General of the UN, had been involved. Subsequent investigation had cleared him of any wrongdoing, but many other high-ups in both the Iraqi and foreign governments were definitely involved. Including, Heather alleged in her articles, members of the US military.

I checked the time. I'd been reading for the better part of two hours. I hustled over to the laundry room and put my wet clothes in the dryer. Then I hustled back to the apartment, and called Heather.

21

"YOU'RE PERSISTENT, aren't you?"

"I guess so," I said.

She laughed. "I like it. Any word from Erin yet?"

"None on my end. What about yours?"

"Not a damn thing. So what's up?"

"I've been reading your articles," I said.

She laughed again. "I'm flattered.

"And I was wondering..." I said.

"Wondering what?"

"Was Erin involved in the Oil-for-Food, or whatever it became once the US invaded, boondoggle? Is that why you're so hot to talk to her, and she's so scared to talk to you?"

There was a long pause at the other end of the connection. "Daaaaamn, you're smart," Heather finally said. "It took me months to get there."

"I had the benefit of reading your articles. I was just following in your footsteps. And those footsteps seemed to be leading to the US military. Which got me to thinking. What if the real scandal wasn't torture? What if it was corruption?"

"Oh, there was plenty of torture too," said Heather.

"I'm sure. But we've already had the exposés of what went down at Abu Ghraib and GTMO. I can't believe what she was involved in was so much worse. I'm sure it would be ugly for her if it came out, but she was just following orders, right? And we got it out of our system already. We had a big witch-hunt after the low-ranking woman who became the public face of a widely implemented policy, sent her and a handful of other low-ranking people to prison, and promoted everyone else."

"Right," said Heather. "And the American public mostly didn't give a good God damn."

"Most people are pretty cool with torture as long as it's not being done to them," I said.

"Too fucking true. You sound like you know what you're talking about. Were you with Erin?" Her voice sharpened with excitement. "Do you know something about it?"

"No," I said. "I saw things from the other side. And mainly in Russia. I worked for a human rights NGO there, gathering evidence of torture and other abuses. So I've never tortured anyone, but I've spoken with a lot of torture victims."

"Fuck," said Heather. "So you know what it's like."

"Uh-huh. I guess."

"Yeah, well, you're right. The site where Erin was working—that was mainly just minor league stuff. None of the really freaky sick sexual shit you hear about. At least not that I've been able to find out so far. Not even a lot of waterboarding. Just your garden-variety sleep deprivation and stress positions. It sounds pretty benign when you say it, doesn't it?"

"Yeah," I said. "Not so benign when you actually live through it."

"Hell no. Sleep deprivation is appalling. But the point is, no one's going to care about that. If anything, it'll probably raise Erin's profile where it matters most to her."

"Uh-huh," I said.

"But corruption, now...we're okay with our brave servicemembers torturing civilians and killing kids, but not lining their pockets while they're at it. *That's* un-American."

"Was that what Erin was doing?" I was having a hard time imagining Erin being involved in a simple bribery and kickback scheme. She was fucked up, but she was, as far as I could tell, fundamentally honest. She might hurt other people if she thought they were the enemy, and hurt herself and the people she cared about because she didn't have any better way of dulling the pain she was drowning in, but I had a hard time imagining her *stealing*.

"Tell you what," said Heather. "Why don't you and I get together. I'm not doing anything better today, and it sounds like maybe if we put our heads together, we can figure out some stuff. And maybe help Erin too. You might not believe me, but I don't want to hurt her. I think she's been hurt enough. She's just a steppingstone to bigger and better targets. And I meant it when I told her I wanted to give her a chance to tell her side of the story. I don't know that it'll help her, but it'll give her a chance to get it off her chest and let the world know what it was like. Because what happened to the prisoners was awful, but what happened to people like Erin was pretty awful too."

"Yeah," I said. "Sounds good. When and where do you want to meet?"

"Hm. This is pretty sensitive stuff. I take it you're not alone?"

"Actually, right now I am. I'm at my boyfriend's apartment, but he's out at the moment. I doubt he'll be back anytime soon. But it's not that nice a place."

"Oh, whatever. You should see the dump I live in. What if I come by around noon and bring sandwiches? Put in the order at your favorite place, and I'll pick it up. Veggie and cheese for me, with a diet Coke."

"Sounds great," I said.

22

I HAD ENOUGH TIME BEFORE Heather arrived to order lunch (veggie and cheese for both of us), finish my laundry, and fret about whether I was making a terrible mistake.

That possibility hadn't occurred to me at all when I'd agreed to her suggestion. But then I'd started to wonder just how safe this was. What did I know about her, really? How sure was I that the woman I was talking to was even Heather Ramirez?

Don't be ridiculous! I told myself. *It has to be her! It was the number Dima gave you, wasn't it? And she **obviously** knew what you were talking about when you referenced her articles. And how dangerous could she be, anyway?*

A quick mental survey of the possibilities led me to consider and reject the idea of her being a serial killer who was targeting me for nefarious reasons of her own. That was too far-fetched to even be worth considering. A more realistic concern was that she might somehow get me to reveal something and then use it against me, or publish it when I didn't want her to.

I debated calling Alex and letting him know what was going on. He'd probably want me to if he knew. But I was afraid that if I did, he and Frank would come hotfooting it down from Salinas and barge in on me and Heather and ruin everything. Either they'd scare her off, or they'd blab a bunch of stuff to her that would be better remaining secret. I didn't know how much she knew about them and their involvement with Erin's problems. The fact that she hadn't gone after them yet made me think she didn't know much.

From what I could gather, Frank had been high-enough ranking to hold real power, and had been somehow instrumental in getting Erin and Alex involved. Alex had, he said, just done the paperwork, but a person who did the paperwork was a person with lots of knowledge. If I were Heather, I'd be after him morning, noon, and night, trying to find out what he'd seen on those boring government forms he'd been typing up in triplicate, or whatever the modern equivalent was.

So what with one thing and another, I decided not to tell Alex and Frank. It would be a fun surprise for them if I found out something really worthwhile. And I'd just have to take my chances that Heather wasn't a serial killer.

When she showed up at my door at 12:03, holding a bag of takeout subs, she didn't look much like a serial killer. She looked like a 50-ish woman who'd seen a lot and done a lot and couldn't be surprised by much anymore, but still believed in the possibility of human goodness even so. She had a body that wasn't exactly fat but certainly wasn't thin and well-kept either, weathered skin with just enough brown to it to hint at her Hispanic heritage, poofy 80s-style hair streaked with gray, just like Tori had said, and cheap sunglasses that revealed big brown eyes full of intelligence when she took them off.

"Well," she said when she stepped inside. "I can see why Kuznetsov went for you. I always heard he couldn't be bothered with women, but I can see why he made an exception for you."

"Um," I said. "Thanks. I guess."

She smiled wryly. "Let me guess: your looks are a burden, and you just want to be respected for your brain?"

"Um," I said. "I don't think that's really the case either. I'm just kind of...me."

She smiled some more. "Fair enough. Shall we eat? I'm starving."

"Sure," I said. "Me too."

I got out Alex's two plates and put them on the table. Heather got out the subs, the paper napkins, and the two bags of chips and two sodas she'd gotten to go along with our modest meal. We arranged ourselves around the table with only moderate awkwardness. Heather, I could already tell, was a straight-talking tough cookie, but she also had that all-important but indefinable quality of "realness" that made it possible to be comfortable around her.

"What happened there?" she asked once she was sitting.

I followed her pointing finger to the crack in the ceiling.

"Earthquake," I said.

"You felt it too? I wasn't sure at first—thought maybe I'd dozed off and was having a hot dream or something—but then I checked the news and yep, earthquake."

"Yeah," I said. "They're still a little scary for me."

"You're not originally from California, then?" She followed up her question with a big bite of her sub, but her shrewd eyes were fixed firmly on me as she ate.

"Nope. Georgia. I'm just here for the summer, teaching at the summer language institute."

"Got it. That how you know Erin?"

"Um," I said. "Sort of, yeah."

She made as if to take another big bite, then stopped herself, curiosity winning out over hunger. "Sounds to me like there's a story there."

"Our relationship is...complicated," I said.

She cocked an eyebrow. "'Complicated' like 'former lovers complicated'?"

"Oh no, nothing like that."

She waited in silence. I waited in silence too. I was good at keeping quiet. I was also worrying again about where I was on the Kinsey Scale, now that I'd just had two comments implying same-sex attractiveness, and that was taking up a lot of my mental energy.

"Oh come on, spit it out," Heather said eventually. She grinned. "I'm going to find out anyway. You might as well tell me, spare us both the trouble of me digging through it. And this way you can control the messaging."

"We don't actually know each other that well," I said. "We met through a mutual friend."

"Uh-huh." Heather looked around the apartment expressively. "The mutual male friend you're sharing this apartment with?"

For a moment I was tempted to demand how she knew. Then I remembered telling her that I was staying at my boyfriend's apartment, and I noticed what was obviously a man's jacket and man's shoes by the door, a man's sweater thrown over the back of my chair, and a piece of scrap paper on the table with a shopping list in Alex's square, masculine handwriting that included items like *Yoghurt for Rowena* and *Cream for Rowena*.

"Yes," I said. "As you can see, I'm living with a man who drinks his coffee black and considers yoghurt to be a disgusting abomination."

Heather smiled at that. "So who is this mystery man?" she asked.

I shrugged. "A colleague of Erin's."

Her smile deepened. "And just how *collegial* is their relationship?"

I shrugged again. I tried to make the gesture cool and insouciant. It came out more stiff and defensive.

"I see," said Heather. Her eyes were sharpening. "This *colleague* wouldn't happen to have been involved in the same stuff as Erin, now would he?"

"You'll have to ask her," I said. "None of this is my story to tell."

She nodded briskly. "Fair enough. For now. I can find out who lives here easily enough, anyway." She cocked an eyebrow at me again. "Or is there some reason I really shouldn't do that?"

I shook my head. "Not really. I don't have a lot of secrets. But I'm also not going to waste both my time and yours by gossiping and telling tales that aren't mine to tell. I really am worried about Erin, and the sooner we find her, the better, for all our sakes."

"Do you think she might pose a danger?" Heather asked. "To herself—or me?"

"I don't know. I guess I haven't completely ruled out the possibility."

"Okaaaay. Then I'll tell you what I know—or as much as I consider relevant—and you can tell me what *you* know. As much as *you* consider relevant, of course."

"Of course," I said. "Maybe you should go first."

23

"YOU READ MY ARTICLES about Oil-for-Food," Heather said between bites of her sub. "You already know a lot of the broad outlines. The program was rotten with corruption from the beginning. But what else do you expect? That's how stuff gets done in most of the world. The only thing unusual about this case was the scale of it."

I nodded. "$10 billion."

"You got that right. Ten billion hard ones. The ordinary Iraqi people got inedible food and expired medicine, and a few rich people in Baghdad got palaces lined with gold."

"Uh-huh," I said.

"And then the US military rolled into town." She paused to take another bite of her sub and wash it down with her diet Coke.

"The program went through some major shake-ups at that point," she said, once she'd swallowed. "A lot of the American military and government personnel who took it over were honest and aboveboard. A few of them weren't."

"Uh-huh," I said.

"I'm sure you've heard the rumors," she said. "People making off with gold toilets and sending the money home to Kansas or wherever."

I decided to vary things up a little. "Yeah," I said. "I've heard rumors."

"And there was some of that, for sure, but that's not where the real money was. The real money was in oil, just like it always was."

"Of course."

"Russian and French petroleum concerns had been getting plenty of tasty Iraqi oil for the past decade, and they didn't want to stop. So certain sensitively placed people managed to do deals with other certain sensitively placed people. The oil continued to flow, and the rest of us continued to gas up our cars with no major pain at the pump."

I went back to my faithful conversational standby. "Uh-huh," I said.

"This is the part where it gets really interesting," Heather said. She put down the last quarter of her sub and leaned forward, her eyes intent on me. "You know of course that we had a lot of private contractors over there along with military and government personnel. Mercenaries, in other words."

"Oh, yes," I said. "I know."

"Blackwater got the biggest press, but they weren't the only ones. And a lot of these private contractors, whether they were providing soldiers, interrogators, or dishwashing and laundry services, were raking in the money hand over fist."

"Yeah," I said. "So I've heard."

"Most of them were making their money semi-legitimately, straight from Uncle Sam. But for some of them, US government contracts weren't enough. They wanted to get into the oil business directly. Or they wanted to cut out the tedious step of procuring and selling the oil, and just take the ill-gotten gains of others."

"Of course," I said.

"Which is where Erin comes in," said Heather.

"You think *Erin* was involved in this? Like, directly? Taking bribes and kickbacks, or stealing already stolen money?"

Heather grinned at the surprise in my voice. "What, you don't think she's capable of it?"

"Frankly," I said, "no."

She nodded in agreement. "Frankly, neither do I," she said. "But I tracked down a few of the people she 'interrogated' and interviewed them. And one of them told me the basic outlines of what I've just told you. He'd been involved with both the old and new version of Oil-for-Food at a low level. He got hauled in for a few routine questions, he says, and the next thing he knew, he was being kept awake by 24/7 pop music and forced to crouch with his hands over his head until he cried." Heather shrugged. "Like I said, it doesn't sound so bad when we're sitting here in sunny California, eating takeout subs and sipping Coke. But it's torture, no question, if it's happening to you. When I talked to him, more than ten years had passed, and he was still a broken man."

"I know," I said.

"Yeah. Yeah, you do, don't you? So he spilled out everything he had to spill. Actually, he spilled it all out during the initial, non-torture-based, interrogation. He figured it would buy him some goodwill and get him out of there faster. But instead it bought him his own personal hell, not to mention a deep and abiding hatred of Americans. I think his son was at a jihadist training camp in Pakistan when I talked to him, all because he was so angry about what'd been done to his father."

"Not surprising," I said.

"Yeah. One of the many little ways we fucked up big time over there."

"Uh-huh," I said.

"Yeah. So anyway, he spilled out everything he knew to Erin on the first, torture-free, interrogation. And he said she got really excited and went to get someone else to hear what he had to say. A man, he said, although he never saw his face, just heard him speaking English. It was the man who ordered the graduation from questioning to torture, he claims, and the man who kept pressing for him to tell them more, tell them more.

"And he would have, he said, but he didn't have any more to tell. He told them everything he could about the Oil-for-Food dealings, and then he started making stuff up, hoping to get out of there. It took him weeks, he said, and he was never able to convince them that he didn't know more. But eventually someone else, some other man, got him released. He said he thought Erin and the other man weren't happy about it, even though they'd already pretty much come to the conclusion they'd squeezed him dry. He says he saw them arguing about it as he was being escorted out. Shouting at each other, he said, almost screaming."

"Did he say who the other two men were?" I asked.

Heather shook her head. "Like I said, the man who gave the orders never showed his face or gave his name. When he was being led away, after he'd been released, he had his back to him. But he remembers the name of the man who got him out. Actually, he's next on my list of people to talk to, especially if Erin falls through. I think he's around here too." She gave me a bright look. "Maybe you know him, since you run in these circles. He's"—she pulled out a notepad and flicked through it— "oh, yeah, here it is. Alexander. Alexander James Miller."

24

I TWITCHED BEFORE I could stop myself.

"You *do* know him!" Heather exclaimed triumphantly.

"Um, maybe," I said. "But..."

"But what?" Her gaze sharpened even further. "What else do you know?"

"You're sure you don't know anything about that other man?" I asked. "Nothing at all?"

"You think you know who he is," she stated.

"No," I said. Too quickly.

"You at least have an educated guess, then."

I started to say something. Then I stopped.

"Come on," she coaxed. "Spit it out. You'll feel better, you really will. It can be off the record. He'll never know you told me." Her face went serious. "I take those kinds of promises seriously, you know."

"I'm sure you do," I said. "But I think he might guess anyway. And...I'm just debating..."

"Debating what?"

"I think," I said, choosing my words slowly and deliberately, "you should maybe give that FBI agent you've been avoiding a call back. Unless you called him back this morning?"

Heather laughed. "No. He sounded like a pain in the ass. I was going to wait until I'd exhausted all other avenues. But you're saying," her gaze was sharp once again, "you're saying he might have something to do with it? That *he* might be the other man?"

"I have no idea," I said. "But he knew Erin back then. And they're close now. *Very* close."

"I see." Heather gave a sharp, decisive nod. "You're right. I should give him a call." She pulled out her phone, then paused. "While you're at it," she said, "why don't you let me in on what you know about this Alexander James Miller?"

"I think you should call Frank," I said. "I think that will answer a lot of your questions."

"Okay." She gave another short, decisive nod. She tapped on her phone, bringing up her call app. Then she paused, gave me a speculative look, brought up another app, and started typing.

After a moment she found whatever it was she'd been looking for, and started reading. It must have been short, because a few seconds later she gave me a surprised look. Then she burst out laughing.

"You!" she said, pointing at me. "You..." She picked up the grocery list from the table. "I take it this is Alexander's handwriting?"

"Alex's," I said. "Yes."

"And I'll bet that's his sweater," she said, pointing at the sweater draped on the back of my chair. "And that's his jacket hanging by the front door. Because this is his apartment, isn't it? I searched for him in the White Pages and it led me straight back to here." She laughed again.

"Uh-huh," I said.

"You weren't kidding when you said your relationship with Erin was complicated," she said. "Now I'm sorry I never asked Erin about him. But I didn't want to tip either of them off about what I was up to."

"Understandable," I said. "And yes, it's complicated. And I really do think you should give Frank a call. Last I heard, he and Alex were off in Salinas, looking for Erin together."

"Yeah." She tapped on her phone again and called. After a moment, Frank's voice came over the speaker.

"McAvoy. Whaddya want?"

"Hi, it's Heather Ramirez. I believe you gave me a call last night, asking to speak with me? Well, I'm free this afternoon, if you're available."

Frank's voice lost its former irritation, filling with that warmth and charm that almost sounded sincere, especially over the phone. "This afternoon would be great. Where are you?"

"I'll be in Salinas soon. Can we meet there?"

"Sure. No problem. When and where?"

"How about the Cherry Bean Coffeehouse? You know, in Oldtown? 2:00pm?"

"We'll be there," said Frank.

Heather ended the call and smiled at me brightly. "Well," she said. "I have to say, this was way more productive than I was expecting it to be. I have to thank you, Rowena."

"Great," I said. "I think."

Her face went serious again. "I really won't go blabbing about what we talked about," she said. "It was all deep background, and I'll never mention your name. And I'll leave it up to you to tell your boyfriend about our little luncheon—or not, as you choose. It's not my business. But I really do have to thank you. The world will be a better place if we can find out what was going on with the Oil-for-Food business on Erin's base."

"Yeah," I said. "I know. I'm just worried that people are going to get hurt. Even worse than they've already been hurt. But I do think someone needs to look into it. And thanks for coming and talking to me, and sharing what you know."

"Anytime." She reached into her purse, fished out a card, and handed it to me. "Call me if you think of anything else. Or, hell, you're bored and you just want to hang out. I like you. You've got depth."

"Thanks," I said. "I'd enjoy that. But I'm leaving for Georgia tomorrow."

She nodded. "Got it. Still, let me know if you think of anything. And look me up whenever you're back in the area. And—I know this is probably a sore subject, but I'll touch on it anyway—say hi to Kuznetsov for me. Like I said, major respect."

"Sure," I said. "Absolutely."

She started to gather up the remnants of our lunch.

"Don't worry about it," I told her. "I can take care of it. You probably need to get going."

"Thanks. We'll be in touch, okay?" She gave me another brisk, decisive nod, and left.

25

I ALWAYS FOUND THAT music helped me think, so I put some on while I cleaned up our lunch things. It was the same Florence + the Machine mix I'd had on the other day. "Breaking Down" promptly came on. Hopefully it wasn't a prediction of the future. Music functioned for me sort of the way tarot or bibliomancy seemed to function for a lot of people: it brought the subconscious currents in my mind to the surface, allowing me to pick up on patterns I hadn't noticed before.

I worked with my hands on autopilot while my brain whirled. I hoped I hadn't done a bad thing by encouraging Heather to call Frank. I hoped I hadn't dropped Alex in a big mess, or put Heather in danger.

The chance of Heather being in danger seemed less likely. I couldn't help but think that Frank could be the other man in the group her source had described. But surely he wouldn't murder a journalist in cold blood, just because she was digging around? He had to know better than most how hard that would be to get away with. And I even suspected that on some level, he had some morals. They weren't the same as my morals, but they were still there, even if buried deeply.

Also, the more I thought about it, the more it seemed like maybe he *wasn't* the other man. Alex had told me Frank had been a hotshot special forces type of guy. Alex, on the other hand, had been essentially a petty bureaucrat, beneath the notice of someone like Frank. Frank hadn't initially remembered him when they'd met again years later here in California. Surely if they'd had a screaming argument in public, though, that would have stuck in Frank's memory.

That suggested—if everything I'd been told was the truth—that the other man was someone else. So who? And did it even matter?

The much more pressing question, from my point of view, was how this was going to affect Alex. Yes, he'd been involved in something pretty bad, but he hadn't had much of a choice, had he? I was aware this was the case for most people who did bad things. It probably didn't matter much to all the people who'd been "interrogated" at that base that the people there had been just following orders. They'd still been tortured.

Maybe some of the torturers had been taking sadistic pleasure out of their actions, which probably did make it even worse for their victims (I knew all too well how repulsive it was to be on the receiving end of someone else's sadistic pleasure, even over very minor things), and some of them had just been going through the motions, but either way, their victims had suffered a lot. I was pretty sure Vasily Grossman had said some rather harsh truths about camp functionaries in *Life and Fate*, and they were just as true when applied to American black sites as Nazi death camps.

But it sounded like Alex really had tried to do what he could to make things better. And I loved him. Despite the current rocky state of our relationship, I was sure I loved him. Some part of me always would. I didn't want him to be hurt, and I especially didn't want him to be hurt because of me.

Think! I told myself as I cleared the table and washed and dried the plates and silverware to the sounds of "Seven Devils." *What do you know? How can you make this better?*

Okay, I knew that Alex was fundamentally competent, intelligent, honest, and honorable. I simply could not picture him getting involved in some kind of under-the-table corruption scheme. I also couldn't picture him not noticing if something like that were happening around him, or not doing something about it once it came to his attention. Granted, he'd been just out of college back then, still practically a kid, with a lot less life experience and probably less strength of character, but still. He *wouldn't* have done something like that. I was as sure of that as I was of anything about him.

And Heather's story seemed to bear that out. It sounded like he'd gone behind the backs of the people he was working with in order to free someone he'd decided was innocent. He'd even gone against Erin, despite being head-over-heels in love with her. Also, I guessed, slightly lower ranked. But he'd gone against her even so, and it sounded like she'd been furious.

Erin...Erin was more difficult. I knew her a lot less well than I knew Alex, and if I searched my heart and told myself the truth, the main thing I felt towards her was active dislike, served with a side of pity. That was not a good basis for a useful analysis of her character and actions.

But I could still try. I knew she'd grown up in wealth and luxury, at least compared to me. Alex had called her a "poor little rich girl," with a politically ambitious uncle and parents with more money and power than someone like me could even imagine. Well, I could *imagine* it. I just couldn't imagine having it. She'd been the black sheep of the family, rebelled, run off and joined up, and gotten into even bigger trouble. She was smart and committed to her job, but also seriously fucked up, with relationship and substance abuse problems. And she'd tortured people.

I tried to imagine Erin taking bribes and kickbacks and funneling illicit Iraqi oil to, say, a private Russian oil company with barely concealed ties to the Kremlin. I had a hard time with it. She was a screw-up, sure, but she was a *smart* screw-up. She'd have to know how bad the consequences would be if something like that got out. Like Heather had said, Americans can forgive torture. Corruption and bad business dealings, not so much. A pretty female Navy officer with a history of drinking and sleeping around who got exposed for dirty oil deals with Russia and France would be crucified in the court of public opinion. Her life would basically be over. And as much as I didn't like her, I thought that Erin, too, had morals in her own way, as well as smarts. She wouldn't dishonor her uniform, betray her country, and potentially ruin her future for money. Certainly not for an amount of money that would still require her to work for a living while staying in the lower-middle-class house she'd inherited from her aunt.

Okay, I said to myself. *So what **would** make her do it?*

I wiped down the table. More grit and dust had come down onto it from the crack in the ceiling. Hopefully the building manager could get that taped up or something. I looked up. The crack seemed wider than it had the night before.

Probably aftershocks, I thought. *The house has been creaking and making noise ever since the earthquake. It's probably still moving around and settling. And maybe we're going to have more quakes soon.*

I started to worry that the building was about to come down around my ears. Then I told myself that kind of fretting normally just hurt me without doing anything positive for anyone, and that I should stop it. I should pack or something. Since I was driving, I didn't *have* to leave early tomorrow morning, but it made sense to do so if I could. I'd start getting my stuff together.

I pulled out my soft-sided suitcase and started packing my freshly washed and folded clothes into it, accompanied by "Rabbit Heart." Fevronia came slinking out from under the bed, gave the suitcase some of the evilest side eye I'd ever seen, and disappeared into the bathroom. Fevronia did not care for car journeys at all, and she seemed to have figured out that there was a connection between them and suitcases.

Why did Erin pack up her favorite outfits? Why did she bring her makeup and hair things? That was assuming Frank was telling the truth. But I thought he was.

Who would she be going to see if she'd packed that kind of stuff?

I stuffed a couple of pairs of socks into the suitcase. Then I pulled them out again, gave the holes in the heels a critical eye, and tossed them in the trash. My wardrobe was not in great shape.

Someone she wanted to impress, I told myself. *That's who.*

Okay. Who would she want to impress?

I considered the possibility of a secret lover. Her behavior did seem to support that. But she was officially with Frank, and she couldn't seem to let go of Alex, either. Where would she have gotten the time and energy for a third man? Maybe it was a skanky one-night stand. But why had she planned it and packed for it, then? Maybe it *was* a secret lover.

She hadn't been planning to meet Heather. No one from work that we know of. But what if...

I examined my underwear. Most of it should probably be tossed too. But then I'd have to go underwear shopping as soon as I got back to Georgia. I stuffed the tatty panties into the suitcase. "Swimming" came on.

What if she was meeting with whomever it was she was dealing with back in Iraq? What if **he** *was her secret lover?*

It was a leap. But it still seemed possible. She'd met with Heather on Wednesday, and sent her away. On Thursday evening she'd been seen drinking alone, looking very unhappy and texting frantically. And on Friday morning she'd packed up her favorite things and disappeared. That spoke of both desperation and some amount of planning. And not caring about her job or her relationship. Like maybe she was incredibly, incredibly desperate—or she was expecting to come into some money, and maybe something in the relationship sphere as well.

Think, think, think! Who could it be?

The obvious answer was someone she'd served with. The obvious person who would know who that might be was Alex. Not only had he been with her, but he'd been the paperwork guy. He'd have all kinds of knowledge about the personnel there.

I reached for my phone, ready to text him. Then I stopped. I didn't want to bother Alex, and I didn't want to bring him my speculations until I had something resembling solid proof. But if the wild idea that had just floated through my head was right, I might be able to find out what I needed to know on my own, anyway.

26

ALEX HAD SAID THAT Erin's uncle was a state senator. A state senator with ambitions for Congress. And it was an election year. A particularly nasty election year. Maybe he was running in a particularly nasty election.

I opened up my laptop and started searching. It took long enough for most of my Florence + the Machine mix to play through again. California only had two senators, neither of whom looked to have any connection to Erin, but it had 53 congressional districts. Searching through all that was a slow process.

But it paid off. The Republican candidate for one of the two districts in San Diego County was a certain Malcom Carver.

Carver was a common-enough last name. He didn't have to be Erin's uncle. He had distinguished silver hair cut short and patrician features that, if I squinted, might resemble Erin's. But that didn't necessarily mean much. *I* resembled Erin, and I was pretty sure there was no common blood between us, other than of the very general Scotch-Irish variety.

I started digging around in his backstory. A successful law practice and political career...community service...happily married to his wife of thirty-seven years...two biological daughters and a son by adoption...son was an Army veteran with a distinguished service record, including time in Afghanistan and two tours of Iraq...

Aha, I thought, and started digging further.

Noel Carver, Malcom Carver's adopted son, had several news pieces dedicated to him in his own right. He'd been adopted by "a prominent San Diego County family" as an orphaned thirteen-year-old. After an initially rocky start he'd turned his life around and had been a star on both the football and soccer teams in high school. University talent scouts had come sniffing around him, but to everyone's surprise, he'd deferred college in order to enlist in the Army.

He'd served two years, including a brief tour of Afghanistan right at the beginning of the US invasion there. Then he'd enrolled at UC San Diego. Instead of getting a sports scholarship as everyone had expected, he'd re-enlisted and put himself through college with the ROTC. He'd double majored in Arabic and Computer Science, and ended up in intelligence after graduating and commissioning.

He'd done two tours of Iraq, including "working with locals, gathering intelligence, and questioning insurgents," as the article euphemistically put it. There was a picture of him in uniform, looking appropriately square-jawed and resolute. Like Erin and his adoptive father Malcom (and me), he had that Black Irish look, with almost-black hair and blue eyes. *Icy* blue eyes, I thought. I hoped mine weren't so cold and chilly. Or maybe I was just imagining things because I wanted to dislike him. I also hoped my own widow's peak didn't look nearly so sinister...I dragged myself back to reading the actual article.

After getting out of the Army, he'd returned to the Middle East as part of a "major private security company." Or in other words, as a mercenary. After a couple of years of that, he'd started his own firm that specialized in brokering deals in the petroleum industry. He was now rumored to be one of the wealthiest people in San Diego County.

Aha, I thought again.

I reached for my phone. Then I stopped, my fingers hovering just above it. Did I really want to do this? Maybe I should call Alex and ask him what he thought.

My fingers descended the last half-inch, picked up the phone, and dialed Alex. The call went to voicemail. I tried Frank. Also voicemail. They were probably deep in conversation with Heather and had put their phones on silent.

Just make the call! I told myself. *What can it hurt? Just make the call and ask about Erin.*

I dialed the number I'd found for Noel Carver's company.

27

"HIGH ENERGY SOLUTIONS," a professional female voice said into the phone. "How can I help you?"

"Hi," I said. "Wow...I wasn't sure someone would answer on a Saturday..."

"Because so many of our partners are based in the Middle East, our workweek is Sunday through Thursday, with a skeleton staff on Saturdays to deal with urgent issues, ma'am," said the woman.

"Wow, interesting...glad I went ahead and called...although I'm not sure if you can help me..." My rudimentary plan if someone actually picked up had been to try to play on the sympathy of whoever answered the phone by acting like a slightly confused, nervous bumbler. Looked like there wouldn't be much acting required. The disjointed sentences were flowing off my tongue with complete naturalness.

The woman on the other end made a sympathetic and professional noise that also encouraged me to state my business and stop wasting her time.

"I was wondering..." I said. "I was wondering if Erin was there?"

"Erin? Could you be more specific about which Erin you're referring to, ma'am?"

"Yes," I said. "Erin Carver. Noel Carver's cousin."

"Can I ask who's calling, ma'am?"

"Sure. It's Rowena Halley. I'm an old friend of Erin's, just here in California for a short time. We were talking about getting together this weekend, before I leave to head back East." I laughed. "She gave me her number, but I must have written it down wrong, because Verizon keeps giving me the 'This number is not in service' recording. But then I remembered her connection with Noel, and I thought I'd give try giving here a call."

"I see, Ms. Halley—is it Ms. Halley?"

"Actually," I said, "it's Doctor Halley."

"My apologies, Doctor Halley." The woman's voice sounded distinctly warmer. "If you leave me your information, I'll see if I can pass it on to Ms. Carver."

"Wow, thanks," I said. "I really appreciate it."

"Of course, Doctor Halley. Any time."

"Great. Thanks again for your help. Have a great day."

"You too, Doctor Halley." The call ended, leaving me to stare for a moment at my phone, wondering if I'd done the right thing.

28

I PACED AROUND THE apartment for a few minutes, waiting to see if Erin would call me right back. She didn't.

After pacing for long enough to listen to "No Light, No Light" in its entirety, I shut off the music app and got out the vacuum cleaner. Neither Alex nor I was particularly keen on vacuuming, and it hadn't been done in far too long. We were both neat and orderly by nature, and Alex had all that marvelous military training to instill habits of cleanliness and order, but we were also busy and stressed out and unhappy. Plus, the elderly vacuum cleaner that had come with the apartment was loud enough it was probably an OSHA violation to run it without ear protection, and it occasionally made strange whining noises and emitted an unpleasant dusty smell. I wasn't convinced running it did any good; in fact, I half-suspected it actually deposited more dirt in the stained gray shag carp than it removed. But I needed to occupy myself with something, so vacuuming it was.

The apartment was small, but I vacuumed every square inch of it twice. I only checked my phone three times. Nothing. Not so much as a text from anyone.

Okay. I could find something else to keep me busy. The bathroom needed to be cleaned. That would take at least 15 minutes.

I'd had friends and roommates, especially although not exclusively of the male persuasion, who kept their bathrooms in health hazard status as a matter of course. Not Alex. When I'd shown up in May and asked if he'd scrubbed the entire thing down with a toothbrush in honor of my arrival, he'd told me, perfectly seriously, that he had, but he only did that two or three times a year. The rest of the time he made do with a sponge.

I'd offered to help out with bathroom cleaning duty while I was here, but he'd still ended up doing it 90% of the time, and whenever I'd done it, I'd felt sloppy and inadequate. But his weekend was being taken up this time with Erin-hunting duty, while I was sitting around doing nothing other than looking for ways to burn off nervous energy. I could do a decent enough job of it. I could even dig out the dedicated toothbrush and scrub the grout between all the tiles, if I got really desperate.

I felt like I'd gotten all I was going to get out of my Florence + the Machine mix, so I switched over to the next selection. That might have been a mistake, since it turned out to be a Miranda Lambert Essentials collection. I listened to Miranda go over her failings in a failed relationship in "More Like Her" while I scrubbed the toilet. By the end of it I was ready to lay my head down on the toilet seat and cry.

You are NOT like that girl! You...

Before I could finish telling myself what I was or was not, "More Like Her" ended and "Gunpowder and Lead" came on.

Yeah! That's more like it. Now for the shower.

I sprayed cleaner on the shower and started scrubbing it while Miranda detailed her plans for dealing with her abusive husband.

Maybe Erin should listen to this. Maybe it would give her some ideas for dealing with Frank...no, wait, I don't want to encourage her to shoot people. I'm against shooting people. Even when they deserve it. Besides, it sounds like Frank is hardly the only person in Erin's life who deserves shooting. In fact, compared with some of the other men in her life, he might actually be a real prince. He might be...

I dropped the sponge, ripped off my rubber gloves, and stopped the music just as the song ended with the sound of a shotgun blast. I checked my text messages and voicemail, just in case something had come in during the last five minutes. Nope.

I tried calling first Alex, then Frank, again. Still no answer. I sent them each a quick text. Then, after wavering at the thought of looking like an idiot, I called up High Energy Solutions again.

29

THE SAME COOLLY PROFESSIONAL female voice answered the phone, asking how she could help me.

"Hi, it's Doctor Halley again," I said.

"Good afternoon, Doctor Halley. I passed on your message to Ms. Carver, but..."

"This may seem like a weird question, but it's important," I said, interrupting her before she could finish explaining why it wasn't her fault that Erin hadn't called me back yet.

"Yes?" Her voice got a lot chillier.

"Is Noel there?"

"Mr. Carver? Is he expecting a call from you?"

"No. But it's important. Really important. I'm a bit worried...no, I'm more than a bit worried he might be in danger."

"Danger?" Alarm crept in through the chilliness.

"Yes. I have reason to believe it's possible that either he or Erin are in danger, or both. Are either of them there?"

"I'm afraid neither of them are on the premises, Doctor Halley. If you think they really are in immediate danger, you should notify law enforcement."

"Yes," I said. "Where?"

"I'm sorry, Doctor Halley?"

"What law enforcement should I notify? Where are they? What jurisdiction should I call?"

There was a long pause at the other end of the line.

"Am I to take it," the receptionist said finally, "that you believe that Ms. Carver poses a threat to Mr. Carver?"

"Yes. And I'm guessing maybe you do too."

There was another long pause at the other end of the line.

"Ms. Carver has always been...erratic," the receptionist finally said.

"Uh-huh," I said.

"I don't mean to speak badly of a friend of yours..."

"She's more my boyfriend's ex-girlfriend than my friend," I said. "Feel free to speak as badly as you want."

A trace of humor crept into her voice. "Well, in that case...Ms. Carver called here on Thursday, just before closing, demanding to speak to Noel—to Mr. Carver. She sounded...upset. As I said, she's always been, well, *erratic*, but this time was worse. This time she sounded positively..." Her voice dropped. "*Unhinged*. I was afraid, to be honest."

"And then what happened? Did he speak to her?"

"He did. And, well, when he got off the phone with her he asked me to make reservations for Friday and Saturday for the both of them at a B&B up the coast."

"Um...where? Which one?"

She hesitated.

"Look, I know you don't know me, and you don't have any reason to give me that kind of information," I said. "But Erin's friends have been searching for her for the past two days, and we're really concerned for her and maybe for anyone else involved with her as well. If you could try to get in touch with Mr. Carver...or call Frank...Frank McAvoy, he's an FBI agent, he's trying to find Erin, you can check him out..."

"Why don't I get in touch with Mr. Carver," she said. "And then I'll let you know what he says. At least he can tell you that they're both all right."

"Thanks," I said. "I'd really appreciate it."

"I'll call you back when I know something," she said, and hung up.

30

I CALLED ALEX. VOICEMAIL. I called Frank. Also voicemail. I called Alex again, and then again when he still didn't answer.

On the third try, he picked up.

"Rowena? Is something the matter?"

"I think I know where Erin is. Sort of."

"Whoa, really? Where?"

"In a B&B on the coast with her cousin, Noel Carver."

There was a moment of stunned silence on the other end of the line. "You think she's with *Noel?*" Alex finally said. "No. That's not possible. And how'd you find out about him, anyway?"

I gave a brief précis of my search for Noel and my conversations with the receptionist at High Energy Solutions.

"No," said Alex. "No way."

"Why not?" I asked.

"Because Erin fucking hates Noel, that's why! Because I had to stop her from blowing his fucking brains out more than once, that's why!"

Sudden voices rose in the background. Frank and Heather, I thought, asking what was going on. No doubt Heather was mentally noting all this down.

"Maybe that's why she arranged to get together with him," I said. "To do it while you weren't around."

"No...surely the fuck not...not after all this fucking time..."

Frank's voice rose in the background again, carrying an unmistakable air of command.

"Frank wants to talk to you," Alex said. I heard the phone get handed over, and then Frank came on the line.

"Rowena? You found Erin?"

I repeated my précis of recent events.

"Nice work. No, really. That's incredible. But you don't know where they are, exactly?"

"Not yet. Oh, wait—the receptionist is trying to call me back."

"Answer her. And tell her I'll be calling her ASAP, too."

"Okay," I said, and switched over to the receptionist's call.

"Doctor Halley? Are you there?"

"Yep," I said.

"I tried to call Noel—Mr. Carver. But he wasn't answering his cell phone. So I called the B&B. They said Noel and Erin checked in yesterday. And then they...they had a noisy altercation, apparently. Well, two noisy altercations, one last night and one today. And the police came around asking for them first thing this morning. They left their room and drove off, but without checking out. The staff looked, and their things are still in their room..."

"They were sharing a room?" I asked.

"Well, yes...didn't you know? They, well, it's a bit sensitive, but they've had a, you know, a *relationship*, on and off for years."

"But they're first cousins," I blurted out.

"Yes, but you know Noel was adopted, don't you? There's no actual blood relationship."

"True," I said. "Any idea where they might have gone?"

"Maybe...I'm worried about Noel...the woman at the B&B said they appeared very strained when they left...and she almost thought..." The receptionist's voice dropped to a whisper. "She almost thought...it looked almost like...Erin was carrying a *gun*, or something."

"Maybe you should call the police," I said.

"Yes...I'm just worried they won't take it seriously...after all, they've already been out to talk to them once today..."

"You should *definitely* talk to Frank McAvoy when he calls, which I'm sure he'll do in a few minutes," I said. "He'll take it seriously for sure."

"Yes...I will...where are you right now, Doctor Halley?"

"Monterey," I told her.

"Oh! Oh, good. They're in Carmel. It's only a few minutes away. Could you go check on them? At least go over to the B&B and see what's up."

"Um," I said. "Okay. Although I'm sure Frank will want to go."

"Yes...how soon will he be able to get there?"

"He's in Salinas. So about half an hour, if he doesn't hit a lot of traffic."

"Yes...and you can get there in half the time..."

"True," I said. "Sure. I'll go over. But Frank's the person to handle this."

"Of course...thank you so much, Doctor Halley...do you have something to write on? I'll give you the name and address of the B&B."

Three minutes later I was out the door, with the address of Erin's B&B on my phone map app. Expected arrival time was ten minutes.

31

ERIN AND NOEL WERE staying at a B&B on the corner of 4th Avenue and Dolores Street in Carmel. It was a pleasant neighborhood full of small inns and big trees. I parked on the street half a block away and hotfooted it over.

I did a quick check of the parking lot tucked away behind the building before going inside. Erin's car wasn't there. I was not much of a car person, but I was pretty sure I could recognize hers because I'd listened to her explain to me in detail how it was a "5th-generation Camaro" and what that meant. It was the only time I could remember her seeming happy. Just goes to show that everyone has hidden depths. Erin's, it seemed, included a passion for muscle cars.

But at the moment there was no sign of her cherry-red Camaro in the lot. I called the receptionist at High Energy Solutions.

"Doctor Halley? Have you found them?"

"Not yet," I said. "What kind of car does Noel drive? Did he take his own car to Carmel?"

"He flew," she told me. "It's a seven-hour drive from San Diego to Carmel—if you're lucky. He caught a flight Friday morning to the Carmel-Monterey airport. The return flight is booked for tomorrow afternoon. He didn't ask me to book a car to pick him up. He said Erin was going to do it."

"Okay," I said. "Well, her car's not here, so they're not back yet from wherever they went. I'm going to go inside and ask."

The entrance to the B&B was through a tiled courtyard full of lush plants and little tables set amongst the planters in a way that maximized both capacity and privacy. It was very nice. I wondered how much this little weekend junket was costing Noel. Probably at least half a month of Alex's rent.

I stepped into the cool interior of the building. It managed to be both shady and light and airy. Whoever had done the original design and the current interior decorating was talented. I revised my estimate of the cost of this weekend upwards.

"Can I help you?"

A woman about my age and height stepped out of a small side room into the foyer. She was wearing a bronze silk jumpsuit that brought out the warm tones in her dark brown skin, neat braids with little silver beads on the tips, and expertly applied lipstick and blusher in slightly metallic earth tones that complemented her jumpsuit. I idly wondered how much she made working reception here, such that she could afford to dress like that.

"I hope so," I said. "I'm here looking for Erin and Noel Carver."

An expression of alarm and distaste rippled across her face. Then she covered it up with a professional smile, and said, "Do you know Mr. and Mrs. Carver? Are they expecting you?"

"I'm friends with Erin," I said. "I'm looking for her. We're all very concerned about her. She just disappeared yesterday and hasn't been answering her phone. But it sounds like she's here."

"Well..." The woman hesitated. "We value our guests' privacy, of course," she said.

"Of course," I agreed.

"And many people like to keep it a secret when they elope and run off on a surprise honeymoon."

"Elope?!? Erin and Noel got married?!!!"

The woman smiled at that. "No one was expecting that, were they?"

"You could say that," I said. "You're sure they got married?"

She hesitated again. "Well...I wasn't at the ceremony, obviously. But they dropped some hints suggesting they'd just run away to get married, and this was their honeymoon...I probably shouldn't say any more. As I said, we value our guests' privacy."

"Sure," I said. "Do you know where they are now?"

She hesitated some more.

"I don't want to bother them," I said. "I just want to check and make sure Erin's all right. It really took us by surprise when she disappeared without a word like that. Of course, who can blame her if she was sneaking off to her honeymoon...but I'd just like to check in on her. Then I'll get out of everyone's hair."

"They're not in their room," said the woman. "I'm not sure where they are..."

A phone rang in the office. Someone answered, their voice muffled through the wall. After a moment, the conversation went silent.

"Jenette! Jenette! Are you there, sugar?"

A woman of at least seventy-five stepped out of the side office. Unlike Jenette, she was petite, almost shriveled, with skin of an indeterminate tan that flirted with multiple racial categories. But she had the same air of elegance and the same large eyes with prominent under-lids that Jenette did.

"Someone's on the phone, wanting to know about special rates for wedding parties," she said. Her voice held a strong trace of Atlanta. "I told them you handle all the special rates. Could you please step in and talk to them?"

"Of course, Grandma. This is my grandmother, Jerelise," Jenette told me. "She came out here from Atlanta forty years ago and bought the place, turned it into what it is today."

"It's lovely," I told Jerelise. "And I thought I recognized an Atlanta accent. That's where I'm from too. Although I'm told I don't talk like it."

She smiled faintly. "Thank you. And no, you don't, hon. Are you checking in?"

"Actually, I'm here looking for a guest. Erin Carver. She checked in with Noel Carver."

"Oh, yes, the Carvers." The same look of alarm and distaste rippled across Jerelise's face that Jenette had been unable to suppress.

"It's actually pretty urgent," I said. "I really need to talk to Erin right away. Do you know where she might be?"

Jerelise hesitated. "We value our guests' privacy," she said.

I nodded. "Of course."

"But that Mrs. Carver..."

I nodded some more, trying to make it look encouraging.

"She's trouble. Anyone could see it." Jerelise's mouth pursed, and something shrewd peered out from her large brown eyes.

"Yes," I agreed. "I'm afraid so. And I'm afraid she might be in trouble right now."

"Some women drag trouble with them wherever they go, even on their honeymoons," said Jerelise.

"They sure do," I agreed. "And right now I'm afraid that's what Erin's doing. For starters, because her current boyfriend and her ex-boyfriend are both on their way down here to find her, and neither of them know about her getting married."

Jerelise pursed her mouth up even more, but this time there was a strong hint of a wry grin in it. "You don't say. Some women...are you trying to get to her ahead of them and warn her?"

"Yes," I said. That thought had only just occurred to me, but now that I was thinking it, I was worrying about how Frank would react to finding out that Erin had run off to spend the weekend with another man, and was apparently passing herself off as his wife. There could be a perfectly innocent explanation for it...scratch that. There couldn't possibly be a perfectly *innocent* explanation for why she would do something like that, but there could be one that didn't involve her cheating on Frank with her first cousin. I understood the thing about there being no blood relationship between them, but still...

Jerelise sucked on her upper lip for a moment, then said, "They went out for breakfast this morning—after the police came by to talk to them—then had a big screaming fight when they got back to their room around midday. I didn't hear what it was about, but I sure heard that it was happening. I think everyone on the whole block heard that it was happening. Some couples, they get married, they think that's going to stop the fighting, but all it does is make it worse."

I nodded.

"Then she went storming out of the building and over to her fancy red car. I thought she was going to drive off on her own, but he came running out after her, and she let him in and they drove off together."

"Any idea where they might have gone?" I asked.

She sucked on her upper lip again for a second, then said, "They were talking about spending the day at Carmel River State Beach. They might have gone there. It's not far. Less than ten minutes away by car."

"Great," I said. "Thank you so much. I'll go check and see if I can find them. And, um, if anyone else comes looking for them, I guess you should tell them too..."

"Even if it's her boyfriend?" asked Jerelise.

"Um..." My first instinct was to say "yes." Then I thought about Frank shooting Erin—in the breast!—and started to doubt. What if she really had been cheating on him with Noel, and had finally decided to dump him for good? What if that's what the original shooting incident had been about? Maybe Frank had guessed something of what was going on, and things had gotten out of hand.

On the other hand, Frank was going to find out one way or another. Better not to make him angry by trying and failing to conceal Erin's whereabouts. I just needed to try to...control the situation. If I could.

"I guess you should go ahead and tell them," I said. "And if they come to the beach, it's a public place, right? Surely no one will create too much of a scene."

Jerelise gave me a skeptical eyebrow raise. "The beach is probably pretty busy this time of day, but these folks don't seem to care too much about making a scene in public, hon."

"Well...good point. But we should probably still tell them. I guess."

"You send them my way, hon," said Jerelise. "I'll hold 'em for a while for you." She gave me another wry smile. "I know how to keep impatient men waiting if I need to."

"Great," I said. "Thanks. Thanks so much for your help. And if Erin shows back up here, tell her Rowena is looking for her, will you?"

"Sure thing, hon," said Jerelise. "Good luck, now."

32

MY PHONE'S MAP TOLD me that Carmel River State Beach was indeed less than ten minutes away. I got in my car and headed over.

The beach was a mile-long crescent just south of the town. I parked at the public lot, right by the mouth of the Carmel River, and headed towards the beach. I passed a cherry-red late-model Camaro that was parked haphazardly in the corner, taking up two spaces. I broke into a run.

There were plenty of other people on the beach. Joggers, dogwalkers, and afternoon strollers moved past me in both directions, at various rates of speed. A group of teenagers was playing frisbee. A couple of sea kayakers were in the water. No one looked like Erin.

I looked up and down the beach, searching for inspiration. Nothing brilliant hit me like a bolt from the blue.

I pulled up my map app on my phone and looked at the map of the beach. It stretched a little ways north from where I was standing, to Carmel Point. It stretched much farther to the south, with trails snaking along the coast beyond.

North or south? North or south? It was a beautiful sunny day on the beach. It should have been an idyllic afternoon for me and Alex, and Erin and whoever it was she was actually with, to sit out on the sand, maybe toss a frisbee back and forth, maybe stroll down to the next point. But the dark blue water seemed to hold an air of menace. Or maybe it was the signs warning people to stay out of the water because swimming was dangerous here.

I turned left and started heading south. North led back to town. South led to Point Lobos State Nature Reserve. If I were Erin, I would want to be away from other people.

I started jogging through the sand. My bad knee appreciated the soft cushioning it provided, but not the extra strain it was putting on my quads and calves. Jeez. I really was out of shape.

My phone *pinged* in my pocket as I came in sight of the end of the beach. I stopped, trying to tell myself I wasn't glad of an excuse to take a break, and pulled it out. It was a text from Alex.

We're in Carmel, at the B&B. The landlady is talking Frank's ear off :) Where are you?

To tell or not to tell? To tell or not to tell? I decided I was more afraid of Erin than of Frank.

Carmel River State Beach, I texted. *Looks like her car's here. But I don't see any sign of her. I'm moving south down the beach, looking for her, but I haven't seen her or Noel yet.*

Have you checked the north end of the beach yet?

Not yet.

I'll go take a look, let you know what I find. You keep heading south.

Got it. Let me know if you spot her!

I put my phone back in my pocket and started jogging again. Slowly. Despite the urgency of the situation, I wasn't in a hurry to find Erin. I didn't like being on my own for this. I was half-convinced that Erin was crazy, and I knew she had a gun. I didn't think she'd shoot at me if she was in her right mind—but maybe she wasn't in her right mind. Everything I'd heard from everyone who'd seen her in the past few days—Zeke and Tori, the bartender at the place she'd been at on Thursday, Heather, Jenette and Jerelise—made it sound like she was on the verge of cracking up. Maybe past the verge. And she'd never expressed any animosity towards me, but I was the woman with the

man she wanted. Or one of the men she wanted, at any rate. She had
to hate me, deep down. Hate me enough to shoot me on sight? I didn't
want to think so, but this was the kind of situation where people did
crazy things. And if she got into another big fight with Noel, I could
literally be caught in the crossfire.

On the other hand, I didn't really want to bring in Alex, and
especially Frank. I trusted Alex to keep a cool head, but the sight of
him might provoke Erin to do something bad. And Frank...I wasn't
sure how Frank would react. If he saw Erin with another man, would
he shrug it off as part of her general fucked-upness, tell himself there
was plenty more where that came from, and walk off? Or would he go
ballistic and trigger a violent, potentially fatal, confrontation? I could
see him going either way.

I'd never been able to get a handle on his feelings for Erin. Was she
just a good-looking piece of ass who fed his superiority complex with
her emotional fragility and the way she stuck with him despite the way
he treated her and her obvious love for another man? Or was he really,
truly in love with her, and that was why he put up with all the baggage
and problems she brought along?

I wanted to guess the former. I wanted to think that someone
like Frank wasn't capable of being truly, deeply in love with another
person. But maybe I was misjudging him. Or maybe his deep sense
of possessiveness and entitlement would make him flip out and start
shooting everyone in sight at the thought of losing something he
thought belonged to him by rights.

The beach came to an abrupt end at a rocky point. I cast about,
looking for Erin. Nothing. But I did see a college-age couple leave the
beach a little farther back, by a service hut, and pick up a trail on the
headlands above the beach.

I've made it to the end of the beach, I texted Alex. *No sign of Erin or
Noel. But there are trails leading farther on. Do you think they could have
taken them?*

We just got to Carmel Point, he texted back. *Don't see anything yet, but we need to look around a bit. There are trails running along the coast to Point Lobos. They could have followed them. It's worth checking out.*

Okay, I wrote. *I'll keep going for a bit, then.*

I backtracked, climbed up above the beach, and started down the trail above it. Jeez. My knee was really unhappy. I dropped from a slow jog down a walk.

I went past a small cove, the water dark blue over black, unwelcoming rocks. The coast here was beautiful, but wild and threatening, with sharp dropoffs and, according to the warning signs, dangerous currents. A child of the Atlantic, I'd always thought of the Pacific as frightening, full of rip currents and sharks and other dangers. I'd occasionally waded in the water here, but never had the slightest desire to go swimming. I had no doubt this was a spectacular area to go diving in. I just planned to take in all its glories secondhand, via TV documentaries.

The trail crossed the bottom of a small but very rugged point. I pulled out my phone. What time was it? I'd been walking for the better part of an hour. The sun was already low in the sky. We needed to wrap this up soon or we'd be out in the dark. What was going on with Alex and Frank?

No texts from either of them. My knee was killing me. When could I legitimately stop? This was turning into a bust. We should stop, reconvene, and figure out a new strategy of investigation.

The trail finished crossing the bottom of the rugged point and came to a much larger cove. It looked like there was a parking lot and visitors' center at the far end of the cove, less than half a mile away. I would make my way there, and then I would call Alex and Frank and tell them to come pick me up.

I started walking slowly along the trail again, concentrating on the ground in front of my feet. I'd pretty much given up on finding Erin, and I was getting tired of spectacular coastal California scenery. I just wanted to find someplace I could sit down and rest my knee and send for Alex to come get me.

There was a loud shout off to my right, from the direction of the beach. For half a second I thought it was people playing. But the shout held a note of alarm that no play-shouting ever would.

I looked over. Then I pulled out my phone and dialed Alex.

"You need to get here right away," I said as soon as he picked up. "Whalers Cove. I've just found Erin."

33

A JUMBLE OF ROCKS STUCK up above the water just off the shore at this end of the beach. Erin and a tall, dark-haired man who had to be Noel were standing on it, arguing furiously. They must have climbed down onto the beach and then waded out onto the rocks. Probably to get away from everyone else so they could have yet another altercation in comparative privacy.

"She's got a gun! She's got a gun!" A middle-aged woman in running shorts and a sports bra was stopped in the path just ahead of me. She had been the one to shout. Now she was peering through the trees that were crowding around the path here, looking anxiously out at the rocks.

"She's got a gun!" she repeated when I came over to stand and stare beside her. Her voice had dropped from an alarmed cry to a shocked whisper. "She's pointing it right at him!"

I squinted through the trees. It was hard to see clearly through the branches along the trail and the salt spray rising around the rocks, but it did look a lot like Erin was pointing a small handgun at Noel.

"Do you have a phone?" I whispered to the woman. Why were we whispering? Noel and Erin couldn't hear us over the crashing of the waves and their own screaming words. But whispering felt like the right thing to do, as if we might disturb some delicate balance by speaking too loudly, and plunge us all into ruin.

"Yes..." The woman's voice was shaking. When she pulled her phone out of the pocket of her running shorts, her hand was shaking too. "Should I call 911?"

"Yes. Tell them where you are, and that Erin Carver is holding Noel Carver at gunpoint."

The woman switched her stare from the rocks to me. "You know them?!?"

"Yes. Make that call. You got that?" I said into the phone to Alex.

"Yes." His breathing was harsh over the phone's speaker. "Frank and I are running back to the car right now. We'll be there as soon as we can. Are you or anyone else in immediate danger?"

"I don't think I am." I tried to look up and down the beach. My view was hampered by the trees. "I don't know about anyone else."

"Right. See if you can clear the area. We'll be there soon."

He hung up. The woman was now on the phone with 911.

"Yes, the rocks on the north end of Whalers Cove," she was saying, her voice still shaking. "Yes, with a gun—what did you say their names are?" she asked me, and held out her phone towards me.

"Erin Carver and Noel Carver," I said into the microphone. "I'm a friend of Erin's. She went missing yesterday and we've been searching for her ever since. She might be...not completely rational."

"Could she be intoxicated, ma'am?" asked the dispatcher.

"Yes. And she's a military veteran with extensive firearms training. She has a concealed carry permit; that's probably her registered handgun she's..."

"He's got a gun!" the middle-aged woman cried, jerking the phone away from me in a convulsive motion of shock.

Through the trees and the spray, I saw Noel raise something and point it at Erin. A moment later, the sound of a gunshot cut through the crashing of the waves.

"Ma'am! Ma'am! Are you still there? Ma'am? Are you okay?"

I grabbed the phone out of the other woman's hand. "Yes. We're fine. Looks like Noel is armed too. He's also a veteran with firearms training and extensive combat experience, FYI. But it looks like Erin's still okay...oh shit!"

"Ma'am? Ma'am! Are you all right? Are you still there?"

I shoved the phone back in the other woman's hands. "Stay on the line with 911. I've got to go."

A group of college kids, laughing and tossing a football back and forth, were walking down the beach, straight towards the rocks. Why hadn't they noticed the gunshot? Oh, because they all had beer bottles in their hands. Those obviously weren't their first beers of the day, either.

The path was on a low headland above the beach. There was no way onto the beach itself from where I was other than jumping off a head-high drop onto rocks. Maybe not the greatest idea.

The college kids were still walking obliviously towards where Erin and Noel were now making irate gestures at each other with their guns. The wind was blowing off the water straight at me. If I tried to shout, it would blow my voice right back at me. The kids would never hear me.

"How can I get down to the beach?" I asked the other woman.

She looked at me, wild-eyed, her mouth open. Probably she'd set off for a pleasant jog along the cove, with no expectation of getting caught up in a gunfight. Now she didn't know how to handle it. Well, who would.

"Stay on the line," I told her again. "I've got to go try and stop them."

I ran a few yards down the path. Jesus, my knee hurt. I stopped and looked over the edge of the trail. Could I scramble down from here?

The kids were staggering as they came closer to the rocks. They looked up and caught sight of Erin and Noel.

Turn around and run! Turn around and run!

But Erin and Noel had both lowered their guns and gone back to shouting at each other. The kids pointed at them and laughed, and then started stumbling towards them again.

"Hey!" I shouted. "Hey! You need to turn around!"

The wind blew my words back into my mouth, making me choke on them. The kids didn't seem to hear them at all.

*Okay. You can do this! It's less than six feet down. There are plenty of handholds. Erin and Noel probably won't see you at all, and if they do, they're probably not going to be able to hit you from that distance, in this wind. You can **do** this!*

I lowered myself down onto my seat, dangled my feet off the edge, and felt for a foothold in the rocks of the cliff face I was going to climb.

"Cliff" is strongly worded. It's more a sort of...drop-off.

A drop-off that's high enough to hurt you pretty bad if you lose your footing and go crashing onto those rocks below.

I looked over the edge. The rocks at the bottom looked unpleasantly jagged. A fall from six feet onto them would be sure to leave me scraped and bleeding all over, and could be fatal if I landed wrong.

Stop thinking those thoughts! Also, you've approached this the wrong way. You need to turn around so that you're facing the cliff.

I twisted around gingerly so that I was face-in to the cliff. Turning my back on Erin and Noel felt horribly exposed. I reminded myself that it would be almost impossible for them to hit me from here with a handgun, even if they were actively trying to. I made myself slide my foot down until it found another hold. Yay. This wasn't so bad. I was almost there. Now for the other foot...oh fuck. My knee really hurt. There. Got the next foothold anyway. And now for the next one...and the next one...Jesus Christ. Had I re-torn my ACL? Argh. Yet another thing to hold against Erin. Another step...is that the ground?

I looked down. Yep. Just one more step, and I'd be on ground level. Still in a jumble of jagged, flesh-tearing rocks, but at ground level. Just put my foot down there, and then step away...

"AAAAGH!"

My shriek of pain and surprise as the rock under my right foot gave away, forcing me to throw all my weight onto my left knee, accomplished what my shouting earlier had failed to do. The kids all looked in my direction.

"Get away! Get away!" I made wild shooing motions at them.

Instead of listening, they came lurching over to me at a half-jog, half-stagger.

"You okay?" asked the one in front. He was tall and muscled and the picture of a golden California surfer dude, except for his bloodshot, beery eyes.

"We have to get away from here! Right now!"

Surfer dude frowned in confusion. "Why?"

"Because we might get shot! Come on!"

"Shot?" He looked around in comical, drunken alarm.

"Yes! Now come on!"

The whole group was looking around wildly in every direction but the right one.

"Come on!" I repeated, and started walking away from the rocks. My knee buckled under me with every step. I bit my lip and kept grimly on. I couldn't see Erin and Noel, but my back itched between my shoulderblades, expecting a shot at any moment.

"What's wrong with you?" Surfer dude had decided to come along. The others were straggling after us. *Thank God.*

"I hurt my knee. Let's go faster."

"You need me to carry you or something?"

"No. Is there a park ranger here?"

"Dunno. You sure you don't need me to carry you?" He grinned down at me. "You're a big girl, but I bet I could still pick you up."

"I'm fine. Let's go faster...whoa!"

I clutched at his arm as both knees buckled under me. *What the heck? Had I torn the **other** ACL? What was that rumbling...*

"Earthquake!" The kids stopped and grabbed each other. For a second they looked genuinely frightened. Then they started whooping and cheering. "Earthquake! Earthquake! Earthquake!"

I pulled away from surfer dude and turned to see what was happening on the rocks. Erin and Noel were both staggering on the wet, uneven surface. That didn't stop their furious argument. Erin raised her gun again.

"NO!" I screamed. The only thing my scream did was cover up the sound of the shot. Noel grabbed at his left arm. When he drew his hand away, it was covered in the bright red of fresh blood. He raised his left hand. The one with the gun in it. If the pain from the gunshot wound and the blood sheeting down his arm was making it more difficult to aim, he didn't show it.

The rumbling grew louder. My knees gave way completely, and I went sprawling inelegantly onto all fours onto the rocky sand.

There was another shot. From Noel's gun, I thought. Both of them staggered...Erin went down on one knee, clutching at her arm...Noel slipped...windmilled his arms...slipped again...and disappeared off the rocks into the water.

34

THE GROUND UNDER ME gave a final ominous rumble, and went still. I pushed myself back to my feet. My hands and knees were bleeding from the fall onto the rocky ground. I pressed my hands to my jeans to try to stanch the bleeding, and started limping to where Erin was crawling along the rocks, calling out, her voice drowned out by the wind and the waves.

The waves were now crashing over the rocks, almost covering them. The tide was coming in. Soon Erin might be stranded from the beach, or washed away entirely. But she crawled along the shrinking rock pile in the opposite direction from the beach, searching frantically. For Noel. Whom she'd just shot at. But shooting someone is different from leaving them to be swept out to sea and drowned.

I looked around, searching for help. Sirens were wailing off in the distance. The cavalry was coming. Not soon enough.

The college kids were scattering at the sound, shouting drunkenly at each other about getting caught with alcohol when half of them were underage. There was a large crowd of people on the other end of the beach, but they were a quarter mile away.

There's no one else! It has to be you.

Gritting my teeth, I forced myself into a shambling, limping run over the stony beach to the pile of rocks where Erin was now crawling around to the back side.

The rock pile was a couple dozen feet off the shore and connected to the main beach by a thin sort of isthmus. In low tide. The rising tide had now covered it completely. I would have to wade out over slippery, water-covered rocks if I wanted to reach Erin.

Maybe I don't want to do this. Maybe this is a stupid idea. They're both crazy, armed, and dangerous. Maybe I should just leave them to do their thing, and let the police take care of it when they get here.

"Noel! Noel! Oh my God! Hang on! Oh my God, Noel! Hang on!"

I was close enough now to hear Erin's panicky voice from the other side of the rock pile. I stepped into the water. Jesus Christ, it was cold. I forced myself to put the other foot into it. Icy Pacific water promptly started wicking up the seams of my jeans. Maybe the cold would do my knee some good.

I took another step, stepped on a piece of kelp, and almost went down. Some rescuer I was. Okay. Another step. And another. Watch out for the kelp...big wave coming in...another step...another piece of kelp...that rock's super-slippery...another big wave coming in...*made it!*

"No! Noel! Noel! Hang on! Hang on!"

I couldn't see Erin from where I was, only hear her panicked cries. I clambered on hands and knees, the rough stone tearing more skin off my palms and shins, onto the rock pile, and started inching cautiously towards the back.

"Erin!" I shouted as I came around the side. "Erin! It's Rowena! I'm here to help!"

"Rowena! Rowena! Thank God!" Erin showed no surprise that I was there. Her face was streaked with saltwater and makeup, a garish, clownish mess with a touch of horror movie monster to it. No gun in her hands. Thank God.

"Help me!" she cried. "Help me get him!"

I sidled cautiously around the last rock between us. A wave crashed into the rock pile. It caught me at full force just as I was inching around a protruding boulder, drenching me from the waist down with bone-chillingly cold water and almost sweeping me off the rock.

I clung to the boulder with my fingers, my feet, my knees, every square inch of body surface I could find. The wave receded, leaving me behind. After a second, I managed to release the death grip I had on the rock and take the final steps to the small ledge where Erin was crouching.

"There he is!" she shouted, pointing out into the water.

I followed her pointing finger. Noel was half-lying facedown on a boulder about a dozen feet away from us. His arms were draped over it, his lower body floating in the water, and it was hard to tell if he was clinging to it for dear life, or lying there senseless. His left arm was dripping blood.

"He fell into the water...and then he almost made it back onto here...then he got caught by a wave and ended up there..." Erin told me tearfully. Even over the strong scent of salt and iodine stirred up by the wind and the waves and the incoming tide, I could smell the alcohol on her breath and oozing from her pores. Vodka, unless I missed my guess. It was an odor I was very familiar with. Anyone who tells you vodka doesn't smell is lying.

"Help is on the way," I told her. "He just has to hang on a little longer and then people will be here to get him." I wasn't sure the police would be much better equipped to get Noel than Erin and I were, but maybe they would have ropes or...some kind of rescue gear that would enable them to get through the rising tide and crashing waves and haul Noel back without getting knocked down or swept away themselves.

Another wave came in, even higher than the ones before. It broke over Noel and the rock he was draped on, hiding both of them completely in dark green water and white foam. Erin screamed. The water receded with a rushing sound. Noel was still there. Erin let out a choking sob of relief. But he was mostly off the rock now, with just his forearms draped over it.

"Noel!" Erin shouted. "Noel! You have to get over here!"

Noel raised his head. Feebly. Then he dropped it back onto the rock.

"NOEL!" Erin screamed.

No response.

"We have to get him," Erin said.

"How?" I asked.

"We have to get him! He's going to drown if we don't! If he falls off the rock...there's a rip current just off the shore here...good swimmers, strong swimmers, get swept out to sea all the time..."

"Are you a good swimmer?" I asked her. I had a brief moment of hope that she was actually a dynamite swimmer. She'd been in the *Navy*, right? Surely she was a better-than-average swimmer, in case of falling off an aircraft carrier or something. Maybe she'd been part of an initiative to integrate women into special forces units and done lots of SEAL training.

"I can barely swim even with two good arms," she said. She loosened the grip she had on her right arm. Blood promptly started leaking through her fingers and soaking her sleeve.

"Well, shit," I said.

Erin almost giggled. Just for a moment. Then her face went back to drunk and scared.

"I wanted to kill him," she said. "I *shot* him! But now I can't bear to watch him die! We...we've got so much history...hurt each other so much...but I can't just let him drown! I *can't*."

"Fair enough," I said. "So how're we going to save him?"

"The water isn't actually that deep," Erin said. "We should be able to walk out to him."

We both looked at the water between us and Noel. During low tide it was probably a charming tide pool, with crabs and sea urchins or whatever lived out here on this side of the world. Right now it was a swirling maelstrom of foam and waist-high water. Technically, yes, it was shallow enough for us to walk through. But I didn't like my chances. Especially if a big wave came in.

"I don't think we'll actually make it," I said.

"We can't just leave him!"

"No. But we have to act in a way that is likely to end with all of us still alive. Otherwise it's just a waste of time and energy. And I wasn't planning on dying today. Alex always forgets to feed Fevronia if I'm not there to remind him."

Erin let out another choking half-laugh, half-sob. "What about that way?" She pointed slightly to the left.

We both looked at where she was pointing. There was a rock spine that ran along the edge of the tide pool, forming a kind of shelf. A shelf of jagged, kelp-and-slime-covered rocks.

"I think we'll slip, go down, and smash our brains out the first time we get hit by a wave," I said.

We both looked right. The water was calmer in that direction. But deeper. Swimming would definitely be required. The water beyond it had an ominous smoothness that suggested a strong current just below the surface.

"Are *you* a good swimmer?" Erin asked hopefully.

"No." I'd balked at swimming in the muddy, cottonmouth-infested waters of the local swimming holes of my Georgia childhood. I had learned just enough at the local public pool to know a crawl from a breaststroke, and hopefully not drown immediately if I ever fell overboard. But I hadn't swum in the better part of twenty years. Now didn't seem like a good time to start up again.

Another big wave came in. When it drained away, Noel was hanging onto the rock with only one hand. He lifted his head and looked at us. Or maybe the water lifted his head for him. Then he dropped it again.

"Rocks it is," I said. "Um...you think you can make it?"

"Do I have a choice?"

"Not if you want to get him back to shore. I'm pretty sure I won't be able to carry him by myself. My knee's pretty wrecked."

"Okay." Erin took a deep breath and squared her shoulders. "Let's go. Um...maybe you should go first? And I'll hold onto you. We don't want to get separated. You don't have any rope, do you?"

"No. I didn't pack for this when I left the house this afternoon. I don't know what I was thinking."

Erin made another of those choking half-sobs, half-laughs. "I'll hold onto your waistband, then. And we'll go nice and slow. And then we'll get Noel, and we'll head off that way"—she pointed along the rocky spine leading back to shore—"and we should be fine. I don't think we'll get caught in a riptide if we go that way. We're practically at the low tide mark here anyway. The current only starts on the other side of these rocks." *Where Noel is* hung in the air unspoken.

"Sounds great," I said. "Let's go."

35

THE GOOD THING ABOUT being soaked to the skin by that earlier wave was that wading over to Noel wasn't going to make me any wetter.

It was, I discovered as soon as I took that first step into the water, going to make me a lot colder. Even if I didn't fall and smash my head on a rock or get carried out to the open ocean, I might develop hypothermia before I could make it back to shore. Noel was probably developing hypothermia already. Between that and the blood loss, it was no wonder he was only marginally conscious.

For the first couple of steps the water was only calf-deep. The rocks were slippery and slimy, but they were also rough enough that there was still plenty of traction. Erin was inching along behind me steadily. Maybe the cold was counteracting the alcohol.

When I put my foot down for the third step, there was nothing there. My left knee, unready and unable to take my full weight, buckled.

"Rowena!" Erin hauled on my waistband with surprising strength, keeping me from going down entirely. Once I'd gotten my balance back, I felt around with my right foot. It found the next step. A foot lower than the previous one. I was now in water above my knees. When Erin followed me into it, it was almost to her hips.

We stopped and braced ourselves for a wave. I tucked my face into my arm as it struck. That kept water from going up my nose and down my mouth. It did nothing to stop my feet from leaving the ground as the wave lifted me up and then dropped me into the suddenly shallow water, causing me to stagger and almost go down again.

"Noel!" Erin's voice was a painful shriek in my ear. "Noel, hang on!"

I looked over to him. To where he had been. For a heartstopping moment, I couldn't see him. Then I caught a glimpse of his hand, still clutching feebly at the rock. His face was half in the water. He was going to drown in minutes, maybe seconds, if he hadn't drowned already.

I took another step. The water rose almost to my waist. When I pushed off for the next step, my feet lifted off the rocks and I floated, drifting right towards the foaming tidal pool and that ominously smooth water beyond it.

Erin's hand on my waistband stopped me. I flailed and doggy-paddled to a rock jutting out of the water ahead of me, grabbing it with both hands and pulling both me and Erin across the deep spot to its relative safety.

"Just a little farther," I said.

Erin nodded. Her makeup was mostly washed off, leaving her face pale and naked, her eyes big with fear. No, not fear. Those were the dilated pupils of a junkie finally getting her fix.

"Do you want me to go in front?" she asked. Now that we were really in trouble, she seemed calm. Almost happy. Like she couldn't function normally without megadoses of adrenaline coursing through her system.

"No. Let's not mess things up. We're only a couple of steps away from Noel. Ready?"

She nodded again. We let go of the rock and tried to move towards Noel, who was separated from us by no more than six feet. Six feet of water that rushed in and out of the tide pool with every wave. We could cross it—if we timed it exactly right. Otherwise we would very likely get dashed onto the bottom of the tide pool and drowned. Or carried out to sea and drowned. Or just drowned.

"We need to go between waves," I shouted back at Erin. "We'll only have a few seconds. Can you do it?"

"Yes! Can you?"

"Do I have a choice?"

She almost grinned. "I can see why Alex loves you," she said.

"Sure," I said. "Okay...the wave is going...now!"

The wave rushed foamingly back, revealing pebble-strewn sand between us and Noel's rock. I bolted forward, jerking Erin along behind me.

My left knee buckled every time I tried to push off from the waterlogged sand, but I made one step...two...my fingers closed on the rough stone, and I started pulling myself up the rock as fast as I could.

Behind me, Erin shrieked. It didn't sound like fear. It sounded like exultation. I looked back, hoping that rescue was on the way.

It wasn't. Erin was still standing in the sand, waiting for me to climb high enough to get out of her way. She'd let go of my waistband so that I could climb. The next wave was coming in. It was higher than our heads, more than twice as high as the previous waves. It was going to break right over the top of the rock. If it caught Erin while she was still in the trough, it would smash her on the rocks or sweep her away for sure.

"CLIMB!" I screamed, and began scrambling as fast as I could towards the top of the rock. My pants tore. The skin on my palms and fingers tore. I kept scrambling. Behind me, I could hear Erin scrambling after me, cursing under her breath and climbing as hard as she could.

I made it to the top of the rock. Noel was below me, just out of reach.

"NOEL!" I shouted. "NOEL, grab my hand!"

He lifted his head. Good. Still conscious. Sort of.

"GRAB MY HAND!" I shouted, stretching my right hand towards him as far as it could reach.

He saw the wave. His muzzy eyes widened. He reached for me. Reached and fell short. On the other side of the rock, I could feel Erin come up behind me and throw her arms around my waist, pinning us both down.

"GRAB MY HAND!" I shouted again.

The wave broke against the rock. Noel stretched, stretched—and clasped my wrist just as the water hit him.

I could feel him float free of the rock as the water lifted him. But it pressed me down like a giant hand, grinding my face against the rough surface of the rocks, squeezing the breath out of my lungs, forcing water where only air should be...

It rushed away. I was still on the rock. Still breathing. Erin's arms were still around me, and Noel's hand was still clasping my wrist.

"Now!" Erin cried. "Now, Noel, now!" And then she was letting go of me and slithering past me on the slimy, skin-tearing stone, and grabbing Noel and hauling him up out of the water.

By the time the next wave hit we were all clinging to each other on the top of the rock.

"You're bleeding," Erin said to me when it had receded. "Your face is bleeding."

I touched it. Ouch. "I think I got a little road rash from the rock. At least the cold salt water should slow the bleeding and fight infection."

"Yeah." Erin looked reflexively down at her right arm. The bleeding had slowed to a trickle. We both looked over at Noel. A red tendril was snaking down his left sleeve.

"I don't think any of us are going to bleed out in the next few minutes, but it would be nice to get out of here," I said.

We looked back towards the beach. It was only a few dozen yards away. A few dozen yards of slippery, jagged rock, crashing waves, and currents that could catch you and carry you out to sea before you knew what happened.

"Do you think we could wait here until help arrives?" I asked.

"Maybe—AGH!"

Another of the super-big waves was bearing down on us. We clutched at each other and the rock as it crashed into us, lifting us off the rock for a terrifying moment before grinding us back down into it as it forced its way into our mouths and noses.

"The tide is still coming in," Erin said between coughs, once the wave was gone. "I think we won't be able to stay here much longer."

I looked over the edge of the rock. The water was now almost twice as high up its side as it had been when we'd set out towards it. Another couple big waves and it would be covered completely.

"So, thinking about it realistically," I said, "what do you think our chances are of making it back to shore?"

We surveyed the path back to the beach.

"Not great," said Erin. "But better than our chances of staying on this rock."

"I hate that you're right," I said. "Okay. How do we do it?"

We both looked over at Noel. He smiled at us weakly. His dark hair was flopping across his forehead, changing his sharp widow's peak from sinister to boyishly vulnerable. His blue eyes, two shades lighter than Erin's and less green than mine, were still muzzy and strange, and he was shivering and swaying as he sat. A combination of blood loss, hypothermia, and a blow to the head, maybe on top of alcohol. Didn't look like we were going to get a lot of help from that corner.

"I think," said Erin, "If we cut across that way, we might be able to make it to a shallow spot pretty quickly." She pointed diagonally towards the beach, to where the surf was breaking on what looked like a shallow shelf of sand.

"Yeah," I said. "Do you think we can actually get there?" Between us and the shallow sand was the spine of rocks we'd just traversed, and then a deep channel carved out by the tide and the waves every time they sluiced over the rocks. It was probably less than ten feet across. Ten feet was a very long way to go through that kind of current.

Another wave broke over our rock, choking us. When it receded, the water was still lapping at our feet.

"I guess we don't have much of a choice," I said. "Unless you've suddenly come up with a better plan."

"No," said Erin. "Have you?"

"No. Okay. Let's do this. Um...how about you go first, and then Noel, and then I'll take up the rear."

"Maybe you should go first," said Erin. "You're the tallest. You have the longest reach. You can grab stuff and pull us to safety the best."

I couldn't argue with that. I was six inches taller than Erin, at least. Noel was my height, and judging by the biceps I could see through the tear in his sleeve, probably stronger, but he seemed too out of it to do anything other than follow along.

"Okay," I said. "Okay, well, here we go. Do you understand?" I asked Noel.

He nodded. Not in a way that gave me a lot of confidence. But it was the best I was going to get.

I looked down at the channel we'd crossed to get onto the rock. It was now knee-deep in water even between waves.

"We're going to have to be quick crossing that," I said. "Really quick. I'll start down as soon as the next wave starts to recede. You follow me as fast as you can. Try to hold onto me and each other if you can. Ready?"

"Let's do this," said Erin. Then she actually grinned, a full-on grin. With all her makeup washed away and her hair in her face, she looked wild, fierce, the brave warrior she'd always been meant to be. I found myself grinning back against my will.

The next wave broke over us. As soon as I could breathe and open my eyes again, I started scooting down the side of the rock.

I hit the channel while the water was still thigh-deep and moving quickly. I lowered myself into it anyway. I was so cold my hands and feet had gone numb, and my stomach felt like it was full of ice. At least I wasn't feeling a lot of pain. Even my face didn't hurt much.

I let the water lift me off the bottom and carry me along. I couldn't swim against the current, but I could angle my movement just enough to land on a rock on the far side.

"Come on!" I shouted back. "Quickly!" I pulled myself higher onto the rocky spine, out of the way of Erin and Noel.

The water was now at its lowest ebb. They entered it together, holding hands. It wasn't deep enough for them to swim, but it still tugged them away from the shore, towards my rocky perch. I reached out and grabbed Erin's outstretched hand just as the water started moving in the opposite direction in front of the next oncoming wave. Between the two of us we pulled Noel up onto the rocks just as the wave filled the channel with a sandy, pebbly *whoosh*.

"Okay," I said once we were all perched there. "Stage one is complete. Oh. And the cavalry have arrived." Police cars were pouring into the parking lot on the other end of the beach, lights flashing and sirens blaring. How could they have only just arrived? I had heard them coming before I'd set off on my rescue mission. It seemed like several eternities had passed since then. But in fact it must have been less than five minutes.

"Oh fuck," Erin and Noel said together. It was the first word Noel had spoken.

"Um," I said. "Have you actually done anything *illegal?* Like, so illegal that you'd seriously considering throwing yourself into a rip current in order to avoid the police?"

"No," said Noel, at the same time as Erin said, "Yes."

"We haven't done anything illegal today," Noel said. He was chattering his teeth and slurring his words, but he seemed more lucid than he had earlier. "Maybe a little unlawful discharging of firearms, but no one was hurt."

"Other than ourselves," said Erin.

He shrugged. "Whatever. You gonna press charges?"

She shook her head.

"Me neither—even though you fucking shot me in my left arm when you know I'm lefthanded, you crazy bitch." He smiled at her, his face full of what seemed like a sick kind of affection. "So, slap on the wrist fine. No biggy. I'll cover it for you if you can't. And we probably shouldn't be out here. Another slap on the wrist fine, at worst. Nothing we can't handle."

"But..." said Erin.

"Listen!" Noel was speaking more and more coherently. "Listen, Erin! The past doesn't matter! It's all in the past! Forgive and forget, isn't that what you said you wanted?"

"Yes," said Erin. "But..."

"But nothing! Forgive and forget, Erin! That's an order!"

"You don't get to give me orders," said Erin. "You never did. Whatever you seemed to think."

"Well, somebody sure fucking should! You can't function unless someone's giving you orders! You..."

His words were swallowed by another extra-big wave smashing into us and choking us.

"I think this rock is about to go underwater too," I said. I looked around. We were at the highest point on the rock spine. The police were getting out of their vehicles and surveying the situation. An ambulance came screaming into the parking lot, followed closely by Frank's car. All extremely cheering sights. All a quarter mile away. By the time they made it to our end of the beach, there wouldn't be any rock for us to sit on anymore. They really needed to call out the Coast Guard and send some kind of a boat for us.

I looked back, towards deep water. No sign of any boats, Coast Guard or otherwise. And the water here was so rough I wasn't sure a boat would be able to get to us.

"Maybe we should try to make it to shore," I said.

We peered over the edge of what was left of the rocky spine. The channel between us and the beach had widened to at least twelve feet of foam and churning water.

"I wonder how deep that is," said Erin.

"Probably deep enough we'll have to swim," I said.

"Fuck it," said Noel. His voice was casual, like we were having a conversation over where to have dinner. "If I'm going to die, it's going to be fighting my way back to dry land, not cowering on this rock. You with me?"

"Yes," said Erin, taking his hand.

"Um, okay," I said. "I guess."

Noel pushed himself off the rocks before any of us could think better of it, pulling Erin along with him.

"Wait!" I called. "The wave..."

Too late. A wave, this time only medium-sized but still big enough, came *whooshing* down the channel, tumbling sand and pebbles and fist-sized rocks at its bottom. It struck Noel and Erin squarely in the side, picking them both up and tumbling them in its grip. They disappeared in its foam.

"Erin!" I shouted. "ERIN!"

Erin's head popped up above the surface. Noel's popped up a moment later. They both started swimming towards the far side.

Okay. Nothing I could do for them. And nothing they could do for me, since they'd left me here to shift for myself.

I can do this. I can swim twelve feet. I'll just be a bit smarter than they were about it.

I waited until the current was moving the other way as the wave was sucked back out into deep water. Then I stepped into it.

It was thigh-deep...knee-deep...calf-deep...it was now the ebb between waves. I forced my way through the water, a nightmarishly slow, laborious struggle to move forward at all.

The current moved against my legs. In the opposite direction. Another wave was coming in. I looked up. Another of the giant waves. The water was already hip-deep, and moving faster, floating my feet out of their tenuous grip on the sand.

I launched myself forward onto my belly, forcing my exhausted arms into a pathetic approximation of a crawl stroke as the current picked up speed, rushing me towards a rocky tide pool. I arrowed towards the other side, swimming harder than I'd ever swum in my life, reaching like I was stretching towards the wall in the gold-medal race at the Olympics, straining, straining...

"Rowena! Grab my hand!" Erin caught one wrist. Noel caught the other. They both heaved, dragging me onto the shallow sandy shelf, where the water was barely above our knees.

"Come on!" Erin said. "Just a few more feet!"

Our arms around each other, we staggered through the surf until we were on dry sand, surrounded by the detritus of the high tide line.

Erin and Noel let go of me to hug each other. I dropped onto my knees and brought my hands to my face. It was wet. With seawater, but also with blood. And tears. The tears had started, and I couldn't stop them.

36

"ERIN! ERIN! THERE YOU are!"

Alex was running up to us. Frank was half a pace behind. The police were approaching more circumspectly.

"Erin!" Alex dropped down on his knees beside her. "You're all right?"

"Alex! You came for me!" She threw her arms around his neck and clung to him as desperately as she'd clung to the rocks when the waves had tried to take us out to sea.

"I'll always come for you."

Frank came over and knelt down in front of me. "You okay, Rowena? Hey. Let's have a look at that pretty face of yours." He peeled my hands away from my face with surprising gentleness. Then he winced when he saw me.

"Hey!" he shouted towards the police officers cautiously approaching. "We need medical attention here!"

"I'm fine. I always cry after something like this. Noel's the one who needs help. I think he hit his head. And he and Erin were both shot. Not badly. But they should get checked out."

"Fuck 'em," said Frank. "They had it coming. They did it to themselves, didn't they?"

"Well...yes." I had stopped crying. I wiped off my face. Ouch. That really hurt. I started to worry that maybe I'd been permanently scarred.

I didn't normally think of myself as a vain person, but the idea of a permanent facial scar was not appealing.

"Don't you worry," Frank told me. "You'll heal up good as new in a few weeks. Mark my words. Hey! Miller! Miller. We need to switch women. Get your hands off my girlfriend and come take care of your own."

Alex jerked away from Erin. "I wasn't..." he began.

"Yeah, whatever. Get your ass over here and take care of Ro. She's pretty banged up. Hey! You! We need a fuckin' medic over here!"

The lead police officer, a brawny Hispanic man with slicked-back black hair and an expression that said he didn't stand for being bossed around by civilians and arrogant white dudes, said we all had to be checked for weapons first. When he saw my face, though, he immediately radioed for the paramedics to hurry up and get out here.

"It's not that bad," I said. "It's the others who need it. They've both been shot, and I think Noel hit his head." Then I had to stop, because my face really was hurting like the dickens. I started to worry that maybe I'd cracked a cheekbone.

The news about the others being shot reminded the police about firearms. Frank and Alex were moved out of the way, and Erin, Noel, and I got patted down and cuffed. I told myself that being handcuffed by the police was a new and interesting experience, and I should be grateful for the chance to have it. I remained unconvinced, though. Maybe I would feel more grateful once the cuffs were off and my face didn't hurt so damn much.

Erin and Noel, it turned out, had both lost their guns in the water at some point. Once the police discovered there were no loose weapons lying around, they got a lot happier, and allowed the paramedics to come check us out.

Alex came back over while the police were dealing with Noel and Erin. He insisted on holding my hand.

"I didn't mean to ignore you," he said while we waited for the paramedics to check Noel for concussion. "I just...I was so worried about Erin...I was sure you'd be fine...you always are....fuck, your face looks bad..."

"It's fine," I told him. "I understand. I would have done the same. And I'm fine."

When the paramedics got to me, though, they made serious faces when they examined my cheek. Their faces got even more serious when I tried to stand and promptly collapsed onto Alex's shoulder.

"My knee," I explained. "I think I re-tore my ACL."

A few minutes later I was lying in a stretcher, being carried back to the parking lot. I had not been at all enthusiastic about being stretchered off the beach, especially cuffed, doubly especially in front of the gathering crowd of gawkers. Some of them were recording the entire thing on their phones. Terrific. But the police and paramedics and Alex had all been very insistent, and common sense told me they were right. Walking would only cause more damage. Plus, it hurt like the devil. I wasn't sure I'd be able to make it without crying. Again. So I let them carry me away. Alex held my hand. He also kept glancing over as Erin was escorted into one of the waiting police vehicles.

"You'll see her again soon," the paramedic on his side of the stretcher told him. "You're all going to end up at the same hospital."

"Oh...yeah...I'll be staying with Rowena anyway," said Alex. He gave my hand a squeeze. He also kept looking at Erin. When the ambulance doors closed behind me, he was still looking at her.

37

I MUST HAVE REALLY been out of it, because it only occurred to me halfway through the ambulance ride that I couldn't possibly afford it. An ambulance ride! Out of network! And the insurance company would probably say that a scraped cheek and an injured knee were not ambulance-worthy, anyway. I could end up owing thousands for this little adventure. Thousands I didn't have. Damn, damn, *damn*.

"Noel can pay for it," Alex said when I brought it up. "He fucking well should, don't you think? And if he tries to cheap out on you, sue the shit out of him. He damn well deserves it."

"I feel," I said, "that there's a lot of backstory here that I don't know."

"Damn right." Alex glanced over at the paramedics. "I'll fill you in when you're feeling better."

Several extremely unfun and no doubt unbelievably expensive hours later, I was released. A detective had taken a statement from me and removed the handcuffs, which was nice. Doctors had poked and prodded and scanned me, and replaced the cuffs with their own restraining devices, in the form of a hip-to-ankle leg brace and a bandage covering most of the right side of my face.

Nothing had been broken, I was assured. The damage to my face was all superficial. It would hurt like hell for a while, but it should heal up with little to no scarring. I'd developed mild hypothermia, but my temperature was already coming back to normal. The knee was more concerning. The ER doctor had bitten her lip and sucked on her teeth when she'd examined it, and told me I needed to get it examined by an orthopedist ASAP.

"I'm not recommending emergency surgery," she told me. "But you might need it soon."

"I'm supposed to drive back to Georgia tomorrow," I said.

She smiled a not-at-all-funny smile. "You're not going to be driving anywhere anytime soon with this knee, I can promise you that. Especially—I hope your car's an automatic?"

"No," I said. "Stick."

She shook her head, and told me to get used to California life for a while.

"Sure," I said. "Of course. That's only sensible."

Now I was back in Alex's apartment, lying on his stained and faded couch, plotting how to get out of here as soon as possible.

"You know the doctor's right, Rowena," Alex told me as he dished up the takeout Chinese he'd ordered. "You can't possibly drive for days, maybe weeks."

"Yeah, but..."

"When do classes start? Not for another couple of weeks, right?"

"Yeah, but..."

"So you can stay here for another week, at least. And if you still don't look ready to drive, get a plane."

"What about my car?" I asked. "What about *Fevronia*?"

"I'll drive them to Georgia myself."

"When? You don't have a break."

"I'll take time off."

"You were just saying how things are going to be crazy with Erin out of commission for a while," I pointed out.

"I don't fucking care. I'll leave anyway."

"I don't want you to have to do that."

"Fuck! Will you just, for once..."

The plate Alex was gesturing angrily at me with fell out of his hand, smashing on the tiled kitchen floor. My chest filled with a deep, rumbling tremble, as if something inside it were breaking, as if the whole world were coming apart...

"Earthquake," said Alex. "Another fucking earthquake!" He laughed. "For a moment I thought I'd developed sudden-onset Parkinson's or some shit like that." He looked at the plate shards at his feet. "Fuck. Let me get something to sweep this up."

The rumbling had stopped. I took a deep breath and wiped my clammy hands on my shirt. It was okay. I was okay. Everything was okay.

"Shit," said Alex. "I think that crack above the table's gotten bigger. And we only have one plate now." He shrugged and grinned. "Guess we'll have to share. It'll be romantic."

"Yeah," I said. "Maybe we should eat on the couch."

He shrugged. "Sounds good to me."

"And you can tell me about Noel," I said. "About Noel and Erin."

He froze. Then he nodded. "Yeah. I probably should, huh? It's only right. You probably can't drink with those pain meds, right?"

"Right," I said.

"Mind if I do?"

"No, of course not. Feel free to grab a beer."

He started rummaging through the corner cupboard, where the remnants of unused kitchen supplies went to die. "I think this story calls for something harder than beer." He pulled out a tumbler and a half-empty bottle of Scotch.

He knocked back a substantial shot of the Scotch before we even started eating. Then he knocked back another respectable portion over the meal. By the time we got to the fortune cookies, he was drunker than I'd ever seen him. Maybe it was dulling the pain on the inside. From the outside, it only looked to be making it worse.

"Okay," he said. He poured himself another portion of Scotch, large enough that I felt slightly drunk just looking at it. Or maybe it was the fumes coming off him and the glass. Maybe it would help dull my pain as well as his. "I guess I gotta tell you. But you gotta promise me...I don't know. No judgment, I guess. No judgment for Erin. She's already had more than enough."

"Sure," I said. "Of course. You can tell me anything."

"Great. Okay, it's like this. Malcom, Erin's uncle, adopted Noel when he was 13. Malcom only had two girls, and he was desperate for a son. So he found a kid who looked kind of like him and needed a good home, and he took him in. So far so good, right?"

"I was hoping this was going to be a happy story," I said. "But now I'm worried."

"You should be. So at first it all seemed to be going well. You know, you hear horror stories about adopting older kids from troubled homes all the time, but there was none of that from Noel. He had a quote-unquote troubled background, but he acted pretty decent, didn't give them any problems. At least not according to Erin. Not until his junior year of high school."

"Oh dear," I said.

"Yeah. He was a star for both the football and soccer teams. Erin was a year younger than him, and was hanging out with him, going everywhere with him. I think she had a thing for him even then."

"Mmmm," I said.

"And then *something* bad happened to her. Real bad. She never told me all the exact details, but I'm sure we can both guess. It involved the soccer team and a lot of underage drinking."

"Was Noel directly involved?" I asked.

Alex shrugged. "I don't know. I don't know that Erin knows. But he was present, or complicit, or something, at least. But it just made Erin even more fixated on him. From what I've gathered, she was already fucked up before then. Like I said, poor little rich girl whose parents didn't give a shit about her, all that crap. And I've always kinda wondered if her dad was, like, you know, abusive. In, like, a sexual way.

Anyway, she was even more fucked up after what happened in high school, and who wouldn't be. But it didn't break her obsession with Noel."

"You think she's obsessed with him?" I asked.

He made a maybe-yes, maybe-no motion. "She sure as fuck was fifteen years ago. Completely fixated on him, even when she was with me. And let me tell you, once I figured that out, it did nothing for my self-esteem. But we're not here to listen to me talk about my problems. And I thought she'd gotten over it. I guess not."

"Yeah," I said. "Guess not."

"Anyway, no charges were pressed or anything, but there was enough of a stink around those boys that their sports scholarships failed to materialize when it came time for college. And Noel enlisted instead of enrolling. I think...I don't know him that well, but I think...I think he felt guilty over what had happened, and this was his way of trying to atone. He enlisted, and then re-upped. Made a whole career out of it."

"Was that why Erin enlisted?" I asked.

"I think so. She wanted to do whatever he did. But she also wanted to prove herself to him, do one better than him. Or something. I think they were on the outs at the time. They...it's like she loves him, and she hates him, and she doesn't know what to do about it. She wanted to do something that would keep them symbolically close but physically apart. So she joined the Navy, since he was Army."

"Makes as much sense as anything," I said.

"Yeah. And for a while it seemed like she was getting her shit together. She started seeing me—and I don't want to make too much of myself as a knight in shining armor, but it really did seem to help her—and she tried to put all that old shit behind her, and...and...and then they ran into each other again. At...at..."

"The place you're probably not supposed to tell me about," I supplied. "The place Heather is so keen to find out about."

"Yeah. *There*. You should have seen her when he came walking into her office. White as a ghost. I thought she was going to pass out in front of us. But she didn't. Instead...instead..."

He took a long drink. Straight from the bottle. I hoped he didn't pass out himself. Alex was only an inch or so taller than me, and slim. On a good day I was sure I could move him without too much difficulty. But today was not a good day. I wasn't sure I could even move myself right now.

"Instead they started...I don't even know what the fuck they started. She kept swearing to me they weren't seeing each other. Not like that. But they sure as fuck were spending a lot of time together. And then...and then..."

He fell silent. I put my hand on his thigh. He laid his hand on top of mine and squeezed it gratefully.

"You gotta understand," he told me. "Noel grew up poor. Before he was adopted, he didn't have a very good life."

"I'm sure," I said.

"And he didn't want that for himself ever again. He was determined to be rich. He was as obsessed with that as Erin was with him."

He fell silent again.

"Did he find something out?" I finally asked. "Something to do with the Oil-for-Food program? Something that enabled him to make a lot of money?"

"Yeah. Yeah. Something that came up in one of the interrogations. And then...then he got Erin involved in it."

"I see," I said.

"Yeah. So...I don't know the full story...but it seems like they were asking people about it...making that the focus of their interrogations..."

"And then you found out," I said.

"Yeah...not at first. Not until they'd been doing it a while, made a bunch of money. Strike that. *Noel* made a bunch of money. Erin was doing it all for him. And I was doing the paperwork for both of them.

I started to notice stuff...stuff that didn't quite make sense...stuff that didn't add up..."

"Heather told me about the confrontation," I said. "Between you, Erin, and another man I'm guessing was Noel. When you arranged for a prisoner to be released."

"Yeah...poor guy...he shouldn't have been there...he wasn't any guiltier than anyone else...he just knew how they could get their hands on a giant pile of cash...Erin...Erin...she...I couldn't believe it when I saw him...I couldn't believe she'd do that to another human being...especially not for money...for fucking money!"

"She wasn't doing it for money," I said gently. "She was doing it for love."

"Yeah. And that was even worse. Because she did it for love for some other guy, some other guy who treated her like crap, who'd maybe raped her when she was still a kid, who was using her now to make him rich. You know, she did all the dirty work. I mean, she was the one running the interrogation booth. She was the one torturing people. She was the one who sold her soul so that he could buy fine wines and fancy cars and whatever else the fuck he thought he wanted."

"Is that how he got his business going?" I asked. "High Energy Solutions? With the money he made from that?"

Alex shrugged. "I guess so. I think he got the idea then, and then got it off the ground when he came back as a private contractor. But I didn't see any of that directly. I got transferred out of there right after our big bust-up. I think that was his doing. But that was okay. Anything to get me out of that hellhole. I went back home and let everyone thank me for my service and tell me what a hero I'd been, and every time I died a little inside."

I ran my fingers through his and squeezed. He squeezed back. Tears were running down his face. He didn't seem to notice. But I did. I sure as hell noticed that here he was, crying over Erin again.

"And then Erin got back, and we tried to make it work, but...Noel was always between us. What she'd done was always between us. She couldn't forgive me for not being able to forgive her. I tried. I really tried. But I couldn't. And it wasn't the torture. I was part of that too. I *had* to forgive her for that. But the fact that she was doing it for another man, so that another man could get rich...that I couldn't get over. And she couldn't get over that. I'd be holding her back, trying to keep her from running off and shooting Noel because she hated him so much, and then I'd be holding her back, trying to keep her from running after him because she loved him so much, and eventually I was just holding her back. And...I lost her. The one thing in my life I couldn't bear to lose, and I lost her."

"I'm sorry," I said.

Alex gave me a sideways look. "I'm pretty drunk," he said. "But I'm still sober enough to know that if I remember this at all tomorrow, I'm going to be cringing pretty fucking hard about how I cried like a girl—shit, I didn't mean it like that—and poured out all my feelings about another woman to you."

"I told you," I said. "You can tell me anything."

"I don't know how I feel about that. I think jealousy might be more appropriate right now."

"I didn't say I wasn't jealous," I said. "I didn't say I didn't want to scratch Erin's eyes out. But I still meant it when I said you could tell me anything."

"Okay." He lifted my hand, still intertwined with his, to his lips and kissed it.

"So anyway," he said after a moment. "Erin and I lost touch. Because I said we had to stop fucking up each other's lives. But then we got back in touch. As you know. And I was with you, and she was with Frank. I thought maybe all that old shit was behind us. As much as it could be. None of us will ever be free of it. Or each other. I'm tied to Erin because of it—and I'm also tied to Frank, and even to Noel, as well. We share this thing I fucking hate that we share, but we *do*. We're kind of...brothers or some shit because of it.

"But then...I only found out about Noel being back in her life recently. This summer, actually. She told me, last month she told me, that he was in California, back in San Diego where they'd both grown up, and they were back in touch. I guess she'd gone searching for him last year. When...when I showed back up in her life. That made her go seeking Noel out. So this is kinda my fucking fault.

"And they...finally got back together or something back in May. Right before...before what happened with Frank. Before the shooting. And then afterwards she turned to him even more. She was...I don't know what was going through her head then, but she went looking for help, and she found him."

"Yeah," I said. "And I'd clean forgotten the whole Frank shooting her thing. It kind of got swept away by all the other craziness."

"Yeah, really. You know, I kept thinking that Frank did it on purpose. That it wasn't an accident like they said it was. It wouldn't be the first time she'd covered up for a man who'd hurt her, after all. But now I'm thinking it was...well, it wasn't 'just' an accident. Frank and Erin are both experienced firearms users. Frank wouldn't just shoot his girlfriend—in the breast! —by mistake. But if they started arguing..."

"Yeah," I said. "Arguing about you, perhaps, or about Noel."

"Yeah," said Alex. "I don't think it was intentional on Frank's part. But it wasn't good either. And it made him yet another man who hurt her. Kinda makes me wonder about myself, you know what I mean?"

"Maybe that's why things didn't work out between you," I said. "Because you *didn't* want to hurt her. She didn't know what to make of that. Maybe she only knows how to be in relationships with abusive men. And then you came along, and she didn't know what to do."

"I hate that thought. I especially hate that I think you're right. So anyway, then Heather started coming after her about...you know, and then...I don't know. I don't know what she and Noel were planning."

"I don't know either," I said. "But, well..."

"You think they were planning to run away together?" Alex asked.

"Something like that. And, um, I don't know how true it is, but...I don't know if Jenette and Jerelise at the B&B said anything about it, but they were passing themselves off as being on their honeymoon. I don't know if they actually got married or not, but..."

"Shit." Alex was squeezing my hand so hard my fingers were starting to turn white.

"Loosen your grip," I told him. "Before you break my fingers."

"What? Oh, shit. Sorry about that. But fuck. Do you really think they're married? Or planning to get married? Would she really do something that fucked up?"

"You're the one who knows her best," I said. "But from my perspective, it seems likely."

"Yeah. Fuck. Fuck!"

"I know," I said.

"She can't marry him. She *can't.*"

"That's not something we get to decide," I said.

"She *can't.* I can't stand for her to marry him. I can't...I can't go through that again...I can't...I can't...I...I still..."

"I think we should go to bed," I said.

"What? Oh, shit, yeah, you're probably completely wiped."

"Yeah," I said. And that was true. But the real reason I wanted to go to bed wasn't because I was tired. It was because I had *known*, with sickening certainty, that if I didn't stop him, Alex was about to blurt out that he still loved Erin. I knew that was true. I just wasn't ready to hear him say it. I'd told him he could tell me anything, but, it turned out, there were limits.

"Let's go to bed," I said.

38

THE NEXT MORNING BROUGHT the arrival of Frank, bearing news.

"Hey, Ro," he said when he came into the apartment. "No, sit, sit. Don't get up on my account. You look like shit."

"Gee, thanks." Although I couldn't argue with his assessment. The whole right side of my face was bruised and swollen, and when I'd checked under the bandage, there was a lurid scrape that was developing nasty scabs. My left knee was also swollen, and couldn't stand having so much as an ounce of weight put on it.

"That's what you get for being a hero," he said. He gave me an assessing look, that unexpected intelligence glinting in his eyes. "You know, I didn't take you for the heroic kind at first. I thought you were just one of them liberal intellectual elites, smart enough in your own way, but ready to lecture me about safe spaces and microaggressions and cry whenever anyone contradicted you."

"Uh-huh," I said.

"But you really came through when it counted. And you might...where's Miller?"

"Getting breakfast." Alex had run out five minutes earlier, on a quest for food. Since I had been planning to leave first thing this morning, and he'd been in too much of a funk to go shopping, we'd let the kitchen get pretty bare. But now that I was going to be stuck here for another week at least, unable even to go out to restaurants, grocery shopping was essential.

"Yeah. Guess he'll be cooking and cleaning for you for a while, huh?"

"Looks like it," I said.

"You gonna be able to make it back to Georgia in time for classes?"

"I hope so," I said.

"Tough cookie like you? 'Course you will. And in the meantime, you might have to come through for Alex as well as yourself. 'Cause I think he's gonna be hurting pretty bad for a while over all this Erin shit."

"Yeah," I said. "How about you?"

He shrugged. "She's hot, I won't lie. I always had a thing for her. But she was stuck on Noel. And Alex. I was always third place for her." He grinned at me. "But third place is still on the podium."

"Uh-huh," I said.

"But looks like Mr. Gold Medal is back. You know, I never could stand that motherfucker. Miller tell you how we know each other?"

"He's told me a little," I said.

"Yeah. Probably more than he should have, but whatever. I don't give a fuck anymore. Anyway, first time I laid eyes on that motherfucker, I wanted to pop him in the fucking mouth. Too bad I didn't, huh?"

"Would it have stopped him?" I asked.

Frank grinned some more. "No. It would have felt pretty fucking sweet, though. But Erin still would have gone back to him anyway."

"Yeah," I said.

"And, you know...I felt bad about what I got her mixed up in. It was my fault. That's what I kept telling myself, anyway. I brought her in 'cause I thought she was smart, and, hell, 'cause I thought she was hot. And she brought Miller with her. Poor guy. She keeps dumping him in the shit, huh?"

"Yep," I said.

Frank gave me a sideways look. "You don't like her much, do you?"

"Nope," I said.

"Good. Sometimes I couldn't believe that goody-goody exterior you've got going on. I knew there had to be something underneath it. 'Course, I figured you were probably a freak in bed, 'cause there had to be a reason Miller kept you around, but I was hoping there was something else as well. I figured you had to be *bad* somewhere deep down."

"Maybe," I said.

"No fucking maybe about it, baby. The fact that you hang out with the three of us means you're bad on the inside, even if you don't know it. And I don't mean 'bad' like 'hot' or 'fine.' I mean bad like *bad*."

"Sure," I said.

He waved a finger at me. "You don't believe me. 'Cause you don't want to believe me. But you were one of us for a reason."

"Okay," I said.

"Only, sure, I'll admit, you're probably not as bad as the rest of us."

"Mmmm," I said.

"I mean...you know what I was...close enough, anyway...I was the hero, the tip of the spear, all that shit...but you don't get to be the tip of the spear by being a nice guy. Spears aren't nice. And Erin...I can't...it was me, you know? I was the one who pulled her into that."

He gave a look of naked appeal. It was so startling I didn't know how to respond. "It was my fault she ended up...what she was. I dragged her into the shit, and I left her there. 'Cause it wasn't me doing it, you know? I just rounded up the bad guys and dumped them on her. She was the one who...you know. She was the one getting her hands dirty."

"Uh-huh," I said.

"And then she got mixed back up with Noel...it's a fucking small world, isn't it? And then...but we thought all that shit was behind her. Until she told me she was seeing him again. Back in May. She told me she'd looked him up and they'd started talking again. Long-distance, mainly, but still. And then...she didn't know what he was up to, she said she didn't know if she could trust him or not, she said he was starting to go kind of stalker on her, so she got a permit and a handgun...and then we went to the fucking range to do some weapons training..."

He looked up at me. "It was an accident, I swear to God it was an accident. It was her weapon. It wasn't loaded. She'd *told* me it wasn't loaded. But...you know, sometimes I think she did it on purpose. She started the fight, and then she gave me a loaded weapon, and then she kind of...bumped into me, and the next thing I knew, the gun had gone off and she was clutching her chest, and..."

"That seems awfully convoluted to me."

"Yeah. It sounds like bullshit, doesn't it? But that's how it happened, I swear to God, that's how it happened. I was pissed at her, sure, but I never would have *shot* her." He gave me a shrewd look. "You thought I did it on purpose, didn't you?"

"Yes," I said.

"Can't say I blame you. And I keep going over it over and over again in my mind. But I didn't do it on purpose. I *didn't*."

"Okay," I said. "I believe you." And I did. Or rather, I believed that both of them had been careless and angry and harboring homicidal/ suicidal thoughts, and a gun had gone off as a result.

"Anyway," he said. "I was just with Erin. Looks like both she and Noel are going to be released. They'll probably be charged with negligent discharge of a firearm or something like that, but they're probably not looking at jail time."

"That's good," I said. "I guess."

"For now," Frank added. "The police don't care much about them, but that Heather woman is all over them. If there's anything to dig up, she's going to get it. And it won't look good for either of them then."

"No," I said. "I'm afraid not."

"Yeah," he said. "Well...I'll get out of your hair. I just wanted to bring you up to speed. Oh, and let you know that I'll probably be available again soon." He winked at me. "So when Miller dumps you so he can keep mooning over Erin, you know where to go."

"Um," I said. "Thanks."

"Anytime. See you around, okay? And take care of yourself, Ro."

"Thanks," I said. "You too." And I meant it. I still didn't like Frank. But I was developing a strange respect for him.

39

I SPENT THE NEXT WEEK growing increasingly restless in Alex's apartment. Frank dropped by several times to check on me. Erin came by once to thank me. All that exultation that had filled her when we'd been in the water together had drained away, leaving her looking even smaller and frailer than usual.

Noel, she said, had gone back to San Diego. Their relationship still appeared to be in the same tortured state of love-hate abusive codependency. They hadn't actually gotten married, she said. She looked sad when she said it. She wasn't sure what she herself was going to do. No one at work was very pleased about her disappearing without warning and then getting involved in a shoot-out at a state park. Her employment might be about to be terminated. She didn't know what she'd do if that happened. I guessed she'd go running back to Noel. I didn't say that.

Heather also came by. She expressed her admiration for my lurid bruising. She also said she was going after High Energy Solutions with everything she had. She'd been digging into Noel's backstory and contacts, and discovering all kinds of dirty dealings with Iraqi and Russian oil concerns. She seemed far too cheerful about it to my mind. Of course, if I were her, I'd probably be cheerful about it as well.

Alex and I spent the week being carefully polite to each other and dancing around the subject of our relationship's future without ever actually discussing it. It seemed pretty clear to me that Alex was now more in love with Erin than ever, even as she seemed to have been pulled inexorably back into Noel's orbit, and also that he hated himself for that. Unfortunately, hating yourself for loving someone often only makes you love them more.

By the end of the week I was hobbling around reasonably well, and said I was ready to drive back to Georgia.

"I said I'd drive the car back for you," Alex said. "And I meant it. I'll do it."

"I know you would. But I really think I'll be okay to do the drive myself." Inside, I was less confident, but I was also desperate to be gone.

"Okay. But if it's too much for you, call me, okay? I don't care where you are, just call me, and I'll come get you, okay?"

"I will," I said. "And thank you."

"Of course."

"You're a good man," I said. "You know that, right?"

"No, I'm not." Alex was washing the dishes after yet another meal of takeout. He turned so that his back was to me. "I'm not."

"You are. Maybe you don't know it yet. But you will someday. And in the meantime, I want you to remember that *I* believe it, even if you don't."

"Thanks." His voice was thick, like maybe he was about to start crying. "I don't know why, though. I've been a shit boyfriend to you."

"But you've been a good friend."

His shoulders shuddered. "Is that what we are?" he asked, speaking into the sink full of dirty dishes. "Friends?"

"Yes," I said. "We were friends first, and we're friends still. At least I hope so."

"So do I. So do...shit!" He'd been holding his one remaining plate as he spoke. Now it slithered out of his soapy hands, balanced for a moment on the edge of the counter, and then slid, rolling and spinning, onto the floor, where it smashed into a dozen pieces.

We both stared at it.

"I don't want that to be a sign," Alex said. "I don't want that to mean that things are broken between us."

"Things have been broken for a long time," I said. "Things were broken before we ever got together."

"I don't want to believe that. I don't want to think we were doomed before we ever got together!"

"Neither do I," I said. "And maybe we're not. Maybe things will work out in the end. But right now things are pretty messed up. Maybe we need to take a little time to fix them."

"I'm pretty messed up, you mean," he said. "I'm still all fucked up over Erin, and I need to get my head straight before you'll want to have anything to do with me. You don't want to get dragged down into all that darkness, all that *dirt*, that I'm up to my neck in."

"It's not like that..."

"It kinda is," he said. "And you're right, Rowena. I'm still so fucked up about what happened with her and what happened in Iraq that I can't do anything else. I can't be there for you the way you need me to. Because all I can think about is being there for Erin. All I can think about is being her knight in shining armor, even when she's running after another man. Pretty fucking pathetic, huh?"

"Or noble," I said. "She needs a knight in shining armor. She really does. I just don't know if it will be enough."

"Yeah. Me neither. But I have to try. For her, and also for me. I have to try to put things right for both of us. We have to redeem ourselves if we're ever going to get any peace. I don't know if we'll ever be able to do it, but we have to try."

"You do," I agreed.

"Yeah. Let's clean up this mess before we hurt ourselves."

I fetched the broom and dustpan. Alex swept up the broken plate, and then wiped up the soapy water that had gotten all over the floor.

"It needed mopping anyway," he said. "And who cares about plates? Overrated, if you ask me."

"Yeah," I said.

He stepped close and put his arms around me. "Do you remember when I helped you pack up in that shitty apartment in New Jersey, and I said I was tempted to fuck you right there on the counter, but I wasn't going to, because I thought it might ruin a beautiful friendship?"

"Yes," I said.

"I kinda feel the same way right now."

"Me too," I said. "Although I don't think I'd be up for anything that acrobatic right now anyway."

He laughed into my ear. "I really do love you, Rowena."

"I know," I said. "I love you too."

"But it's not enough, is it? It's not the right kind of love, is it?"

"Not right now," I said. "Who knows what it will be in the future. You know, I've been thinking about how what you felt for Erin was a kind of lightning-strike love. And it sounds like what she has for Noel is lightning-strike love too, in its own sick way. And I've had my own brushes with lightning in the past as well. So now we're all singed and scarred, and we're looking for love without the lightning. But we need it in order to function. We're like the forests here out West: we need lightning strikes and wildfires in order to stay healthy. And right now maybe what we need is a lot of fire to burn away all the old bad brush and clear things out so that we can start growing again."

Alex's arms tightened around me. "I like that thought. We haven't ruined things. We're just...waiting for things to go right. Like fine wine, or something. Or a forest, like you said, waiting for lightning to strike and the rain to come down, so that it can grow."

"Yeah," I said. "We haven't ruined anything at all."

40

I SET OFF EARLY THE next morning. Alex stood and watched me drive away, after making me promise three times that I'd call him if I had so much as a twinge of doubt about my ability to make it back to Georgia. He'd drop everything, he promised, and come get me.

I'd promised that I'd do so. And I meant it. But I really hoped it wasn't necessary. I'd also meant it when I'd said that I didn't think things were broken forever between us, and we were still friends, and maybe one day we would be more than that again.

Right now, though, I felt raw and sore inside. Burned, one might say. Because while I'd meant all that, I also knew that it wasn't the whole story. Alex had a journey he had to take, and it seemed he wouldn't be able to do it with me by his side. Everyone deserved a shot at redemption, and maybe Alex would take his someday, but not with me, not with me. The pain from that thought was worse than I would have expected.

And maybe I had my own problems I needed to face. Maybe all my doubts about what kind of love I felt for Alex and what kind of future we had, and where I was on the Kinsey Scale, and all that kind of stuff, weren't really about love at all. Maybe they were about the fact that deep down, I thought Frank was right. Deep down, I thought I was *bad*, just like him and Alex and Noel and Erin.

Or maybe I wanted to be a part of that badness. Maybe my need to help people was a way to touch that badness without letting it claim me. Dima and Alex had both said they wanted to protect me from the dirt and darkness and danger that had damaged them so badly. But maybe I needed it. I needed something to balance out all the goodness I wore on the outside. I was pretty sure the goodness was real. But it seemed to crave contact with real badness, like I could only function if there was some kind of Manichean battle between good and evil going on inside me. And right now, I wasn't sure it was a battle I could win.

Don't cry! I ordered myself. *You'll be a traffic hazard.*

I brought up my music app on my phone while stopped at a light. "More Like Her" came on.

No, no, no!

I brought up another playlist. "Shake it Out" started playing. Okay, this was better. The light turned green and I pulled forward.

It was followed by "Never Let Me Go."

NO! Clearly this isn't working.

At the next light I shut off my music app and turned on the radio to a random station. There was a report about traffic, followed by some banter by the hosts. Ugh. I hated morning drive-time radio host banter.

"And now, said the male host, just as I was reaching for the dial to change the station, "let's go back to 1982. Shelley, do you remember what you were doing in 1982?"

"Being born," said Shelley.

Both hosts laughed.

"Well, for those of us with a little more experience with the world, this song will bring back happy memories. Maybe it'll bring back happy memories for your parents, Shelley. I bet if you ask 'em, they'll tell you this album had something to do with you being born, or at least what happened nine months earlier."

"Maybe," said Shelley, with the voice of a woman trying to be a good sport.

"So here we go, ladies and gentlemen. 'Gypsy,' by Fleetwood Mac. Let the memories come rolling back!"

The song started playing. I knew it. I just hadn't thought about it in a long time. But right now, as I was driving through this not very nice part of California, leaving behind a man I loved and who loved me, but not enough to be with me, and heading towards somewhere I didn't really want to go, it seemed like the perfect song. I didn't even know why. It just did.

Because lightning strikes, I told myself. *Sometimes it only strikes once, sometimes it strikes twice, but it **does** strike. And sometimes when it does, it brings cleansing, not destruction. You just have to be in the right place at the right time for it to hit you.*

I drove for a couple of hours before stopping for a break. So far my knee was holding up pretty well. I had a long way to go, but I was starting to feel optimistic that I would get there.

A message popped up on my phone as I was getting back in the car.

Darling Inna, it said. *Mama has agreed to try treatment in America. She is insisting that I come with her))) We are starting the process of getting visas. We may be with you in America this winter. Hugs and kisses, Dima.*

The End

*WANT TO KNOW WHAT HAPPENS next? Grab **Under Review**, book 7 in the Doctor Rowena Halley series, by scanning the QR code below:*

AND IF YOU WANT TO stay in touch *and* get a free novella, you can join my mailing list by scanning the QR code below:

Author's Note

WHILE *Total Immersion* is fiction, like all the books in the Doctor Rowena Halley series, it has a basis in fact.

The Oil-for-Food program was real, as was the $10 Billion in bribes and kickbacks that was collected around it. The involvement of individuals from the US military in using it for personal gain following the 2003 invasion is a product of my own imagination—as far as I know.

The US program of "enhanced interrogation" at black sites in Iraq and other places has been extensively documented. The book *Consequence: A Memoir* by Eric Fair, about an interrogator in Iraq, is an excellent look into how good people found themselves doing bad things. *Enhanced Interrogation: Inside the Minds and Motives of the Islamic Terrorists Trying to Destroy America*, by James E. Mitchell and Bill Harlow, provides an insider account of the creation of the program of enhanced interrogation by one of its founders. *The Lonely Soldier: The Private War of Women Serving in Iraq*, by Helen Benedict, has stories of women serving during the early years of the invasion and their struggles, including the experiences of female MPs guarding prisoners.

A useful book on the war from a journalist's perspective is *War Journal: My Five Years in Iraq*, by Richard Engel, the Middle East Bureau Chief for NBC News. And *Blackwater: The Rise of the World's Most Powerful Mercenary Army*, by Jeremy Scahill, is a gripping exposé of the actions of private contractors in the war.

All the places described in the story are based on real locations, although I may have taken some liberties in some instances to raise the excitement level!

Once again, I owe a debt of gratitude to the WRITERSDETECTIVE Q&A Facebook group and the Writer's Detective Bureau podcast for patiently answering my questions about police procedure. All of these sources have been very helpful during the writing of this book. All errors and inaccuracies are, of course, my own.

Sid Stark

About the Author

SID STARK LIVES A LIFE very similar to her characters', only with more grading and fewer exciting chase scenes. She did once get held up in Heathrow on suspicion of being a Russian criminal traveling on an American passport, though, which was fun. She loves to hear from her readers, and can be reached by email at **sidstark@sidstarkauthor.com,** at her website at **https://sidstarkauthor.com/,** on Facebook at **https://www.facebook.com/SidStarkAuthor/,** and Twitter at **@SidStarkAuthor.**

Don't miss out!

Visit the website below and you can sign up to receive emails whenever Sid Stark publishes a new book. There's no charge and no obligation.

https://books2read.com/r/B-A-NVEK-IACQB

BOOKS 2 READ

Connecting independent readers to independent writers.

Also by Sid Stark

Doctor Rowena Halley

Campus Confidential: An Academic Thriller
Permanent Position: An Academic Thriller
Summer Session: An Academic Thriller
Trigger Warning: An Academic Thriller
Honor Court: An Academic Thriller
Total Immersion: An Academic Thriller
Under Review: An Academic Thriller

Doctor Rowena Halley Boxed Sets

The Doctor Rowena Halley Series Books 1-4: Four Dark Comedy
Mysteries